"I Asked One Thing Of You, Julianne. One. To Stay Out Of This Room. You Disobeyed."

"I was going to tell you tonight. I—"

"Your trespassing has consequences. Huge ones. Far-reaching." He shoved his hands through his hair.

"I don't even know what all this means," she said, sweeping the room with her gaze. An almost hysterical laugh escaped her, small and shaky. "I'm sorry I violated your trust, but—"

"Sorry? Yes, I'm sure you are, and about to become more so." He put a hand under her chin and lifted her face toward him. "Because now you have to marry me."

Dear Reader,

Things are heating up in our family dynasty series, THE ELLIOTTS, with *Heiress Beware* by Charlene Sands. Seems the rich girl has gotten herself into a load of trouble and has ended up in the arms of a sexy Montana stranger. (Well...there are worse things that could happen.)

We've got miniseries galore this month, as well. There's the third book in Maureen Child's wonderful SUMMER OF SECRETS series, *Satisfying Lonergan's Honor,* in which the hero learns a startling fifteen-year-old secret. And our high-society continuity series, SECRET LIVES OF SOCIETY WIVES, features *The Soon-To-Be-Disinherited Wife* by Jennifer Greene. Also, Emilie Rose launches a brand-new trilogy about three socialites who use their trust funds to purchase bachelors at a charity auction. TRUST FUND AFFAIRS gets kicked off right with *Paying the Playboy's Price.*

June also brings us the second title in our RICH AND RECLUSIVE series, which focuses on wealthy, mysterious men. *Forced to the Altar,* Susan Crosby's tale of a woman at the mercy of a...yes...wealthy, mysterious man, will leave you breathless. And rounding out the month is Cindy Gerard's emotional tale of a pregnant heroine who finds a knight in shining armor with *A Convenient Proposition.*

So start your summer off right with all the delectable reads from Silhouette Desire.

Happy reading!

Melissa Jeglinski

Melissa Jeglinski
Senior Editor
Silhouette Books

Please address questions and book requests to:
Silhouette Reader Service
U.S.: 3010 Walden Ave., P.O. Box 1325, Buffalo, NY 14269
Canadian: P.O. Box 609, Fort Erie, Ont. L2A 5X3

SUSAN CROSBY

Forced
to the Altar

Published by Silhouette Books
America's Publisher of Contemporary Romance

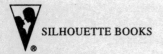

SILHOUETTE BOOKS

ISBN 0-373-76733-1

FORCED TO THE ALTAR

Copyright © 2006 by Susan Bova Crosby

Visit Silhouette Books at www.eHarlequin.com

Printed in U.S.A.

Books by Susan Crosby

Silhouette Desire

The Mating Game #888
Almost a Honeymoon #952
Baby Fever #1018
Wedding Fever #1061
Marriage on His Mind #1108
Bride Candidate #9 #1131
His Most Scandalous Secret #1158
His Seductive Revenge #1162
His Ultimate Temptation #1186
The Groom's Revenge #1214
The Baby Gift #1301
†*Christmas Bonus, Strings Attached* #1554

†*Private Indiscretions* #1570
†*Hot Contact* #1590
†*Rules of Attraction* #1647
†*Heart of the Raven* #1653
†*Secrets of Paternity* #1659
The Forbidden Twin #1717
Forced to the Altar #1733

*The Lone Wolves
†Behind Closed Doors

SUSAN CROSBY

believes in the value of setting goals, but also in the magic of making wishes. A longtime reader of romance novels, Susan earned a B.A. in English while raising her sons. She lives in the central valley of California, the land of wine grapes, asparagus and almonds. Her checkered past includes jobs as a synchronized swimming instructor, personnel interviewer at a toy factory and trucking company manager, but her current occupation as a writer is her all-time favorite.

Susan enjoys writing about people who take a chance on love, sometimes against all odds. She loves warm, strong heroes; good-hearted, self-reliant heroines...and happy endings.

Susan loves to hear from readers. You can visit her at her Web site, www.susancrosby.com.

To my sisters of the Sacramento Valley Rose—for your love and support, your never-ending passion to achieve and your constant good cheer. You are the best!

One

"This was not part of the plan," Julianne Johnson muttered, the words swallowed by the drone of a speedboat as it raced toward Promontory, one of the San Juan Islands off the Washington coast. According to the Internet, the islands were tourist havens dotted with fishing villages, artist colonies and bicycle paths. But not Promontory—or the Prom, as the boat pilot called it—which was accessible only by private boat or helicopter, not a public ferry.

She studied the approaching island. How could it be so isolated and have tourists? Although she'd been sent here to lay low during her brother's trial, she would earn her keep by working for the owner of the Spirit Inn, Zach Keller. If there was an inn, there must be visitors, right?

Maybe it wouldn't be as lonely as she pictured.

"Where's the town?" she shouted to the pilot, Mr.

Moody, a sixtyish man with gunmetal gray hair and a muscular physique.

He pointed ahead. She saw nothing but trees, crags and a steep, rugged rock—a promontory—projecting into the Pacific Ocean.

Purgatory seemed like a more appropriate description to the twenty-three-year-old, Southern California, land-of-sunshine-and-malls girl about to be imprisoned by water, and without decent shopping.

And she was stuck there.

The boat slowed abruptly then eased into a slip alongside others, evidence that other human beings inhabited the island.

Mr. Moody secured the craft then offered her a hand up to the floating dock, which swayed and pitched as she moved toward the landing. A Jeep was parked nearby; otherwise, she saw no signs of life.

"Where is the town?" Julianne asked again.

"Yonder," he said cocking his head, a suitcase of hers in each hand.

"What's there?"

"General store. A gas pump."

"That's it?"

"Don't need more'n that."

They drove up a narrow, paved road. Within a couple of minutes, a structure appeared in the distance. She watched in increasing awe as the details came into focus. "It's a castle," she murmured, delighted.

"Brought stone by stone from Scotland then reassembled."

"By Mr. Keller?" She created a picture of her new boss, wearing plaid, his red hair wind-tossed by the ocean breezes.

"Nope. Someone long ago, Angus McMahon." Mr. Moody pulled up beside the building.

They climbed out of the vehicle and approached a stone archway sheltering a solid wood door. The late November gloom kept partner with them as they stepped into the castle. Gray stone walls and floors echoed their footsteps as Julianne followed him from a utility room into a space with a large open hearth, but otherwise a modern kitchen, with stainless steel fixtures and granite countertops.

A tall, sturdy woman with bright red hair stood at the sink washing lettuce. She didn't quite smile.

"My wife, Iris," Mr. Moody said.

"Welcome, Miss Johnson."

"Julianne, please," she said, testing her new name, her in-hiding name.

She hoped the couple would extend her the same courtesy, but neither of them asked her to call them by their first names. She wondered whether she should've chosen a different place to hide out, someplace a little more casual. Not that she'd been given a choice, since her supposed-friend James Paladin, Jamey, had arranged it without presenting any options.

"I'll show you to your room," Mrs. Moody said, wiping her hands on her apron and taking one suitcase from her husband.

Julianne reached for the other and followed. They climbed two flights, up narrow stairwells that felt as if they should have been full of spiderwebs but, in truth, were spotless. The illusion gave her the creeps. At the top was a narrow landing and a door, and that was all. One door. No hallway leading to anywhere else.

"This is one of two tower rooms," Mrs. Moody said. She set Julianne's suitcase on a wooden chest at the foot of a massive four-poster bed topped with a fluffy burgundy comforter and mounded with pillows. "The clothes you sent last week have been put away in the wardrobe and the dresser."

Julianne winced at the thought of a stranger handling her clothes.

"The castle was renovated a few years back. You'll find all the comforts of home. Extra blankets are under the window seat. After you're settled, come to the kitchen. Mr. Zach will not be joining you for dinner. He's sleeping."

Sleeping? He must be very old to be napping at six o'clock in the evening, Julianne figured. "Thank you, Mrs. Moody."

The woman closed the door behind herself as Julianne turned in a slow circle. Large tapestries hung on two walls. A tall, narrow window drew her. She knelt on the window seat, but night had settled, and she couldn't see much except the silhouettes of trees and rocks.

She'd only lived in cities, although always near the ocean. She welcomed the sharp, salty scent of the air, and the breezes, sometimes violent, sometimes gentle, but the air rarely stagnant. She did not, however, enjoy isolation. She could only hope that her brother's case would go to trial soon and be done with quickly. That day of emancipation would be a welcome one. She had plans—finish college, live life in her own way, not as someone told her she must. Independence. She couldn't wait.

Until then, she should be grateful Jamey had found her a safe place to wait out the storm…

So, why then, didn't she feel very safe?

* * *

Julianne approached a massive, wood dining table that easily seated twelve in the high-back, richly upholstered chairs, reminiscent of another century. The single place setting at one end meant she didn't have to guess where to sit.

"I'm not a guest," she protested to Mrs. Moody, who had led the way to the dining room, a tray in hand. "I can eat with you and Mr. Moody."

"We dined earlier."

Julianne bit back a sigh. Some surprising obstacles faced her in her new situation—a boss who apparently slept a lot, two protective and barely sociable fellow employees, and more isolation than Jamey had led her to believe.

"There aren't any guests?" Julianne asked.

"This is not a popular time of year to vacation on the Prom. Enjoy your meal."

The tasty fish stew, green salad and crunchy bread satisfied Julianne's hunger for food but not for company. She could even hear herself chew. And strange sounds from above, bumps in the night, startled her. She finished in a hurry and returned her tray to the kitchen, where she found Mr. and Mrs. Moody sitting at a small table, sipping tea.

"That was so good, thank you, Mrs. Moody," Julianne said, setting the tray on the counter, then plopping the dishes into a sink mounded with soap bubbles. "No, don't get up. I'll do them." She plunged her hands in the hot water and looked over her shoulder. "What do you do for entertainment?"

"You'll find a big-screen TV in the media room. There's a satellite dish, DVD player and an extensive library of movies."

Julianne glanced at her watch. It was barely seven-thirty, too early to retire to her room, even after her long day of travel.

"Would you give me a tour of the house when I'm done?" she asked.

The couple stood. "My husband will take you." Mrs. Moody nudged Julianne aside, taking over at the sink. "I will see you in the morning. Coffee is ready by 6:00 a.m., but of course you may take your time. You won't punch a time clock here."

"Thank you." She was used to getting up early, had reported for work at 6:00 a.m. at her last job waiting tables.

Mr. Moody led her through the dining room and across a wide hallway and entry hall into a substantial living room that included a huge fireplace, a grand piano—she couldn't imagine how they'd transported the instrument up the hill and into the castle—and furnishings of a style Julianne guessed was nineteenth century.

Next was the media room, modern in both technology and furnishings, yet not jarringly out of place.

"That's Mr. Zach's office," Mr. Moody said, pointing to a door farther down the hall. "You're not to enter it."

Why not?

A bathroom, guest room and the Moodys' suite rounded out the bottom floor. Julianne and Mr. Moody circled back to the entry hall, which contained a substantial staircase that ascended to the second level.

"Only one room up here concerns you," he said as they reached the landing and turned right. "This room. It'll be your work space."

"May I see the other tower room?" she asked. "Does it look the same as mine?"

"It's locked." He opened the door to her office then stepped aside, allowing her to enter. The room held a computer and rows of file cabinets. At least it looked like she might have work to do.

A few minutes later, Mr. Moody left her in the media room. She surfed the more-than-a-hundred channels on the satellite-dish network, then settled on a DVD, *Legally Blonde*, which she hoped would make her laugh.

The movie proved not to be a distraction, and she turned it off after an hour. Low-light sconces on the walls guided her way to her room, where she sat cross-legged on the window seat. Out of the corner of her eye she saw movement. The half moon didn't make much of a spotlight, but it was enough to cast a man in silhouette walking along the bluff, the only place where trees didn't grow. In her imagination, an aura of darkness surrounded him—dark hair and eyes, a forbidding expression.

Since the castle seemed to be the only structure on this end of the island, she guessed it was her benefactor, Zach Keller. If he was old, he still had a full head of hair—it and his long coat blew behind him in the wind.

Hope swelled in her—hope that he would be kind and honest, that he would make her laugh. She needed to laugh.

He stopped and turned toward the castle. She drew back as the light from her room, even from such a distance, probably revealed her sitting in the window seat watching him. After a minute she turned out her light then resettled on the seat, feeling like a spy, but in need of entertainment.

Two large dogs raced by the man, their strides long and quick. They skidded to a stop, then bounded back to him, bumping against his legs as he leaned over to pet them.

Her cell phone rang. Her heart pounded, as if she'd been caught spying red-handed.

"Hello, Jamey," she said to the only person who knew the number of her new satellite cell phone.

"You made it okay?"

"I'm here." She sat on the window seat again and looked outdoors, but the man and dogs were gone. "I'm not sure if sending me here was a favor."

"A little rustic for your taste, Venus?"

"Julianne," she said, reminding him of her new name. "You told me I would be safe here. You didn't tell me I would be stuck in the middle of nowhere. And, frankly, this place is a little creepy."

"You said you wanted to disappear. Like your mother. Those were your exact words."

"And you said that this Zach Keller needs me. You'd better be right about that. There'd better be a ton of work to do, because I'm already going stir crazy."

"There are needs, and then there are needs, Julianne."

That silenced her for a few seconds. "Meaning what? I haven't even met the man yet."

"You'll see for yourself, if it's meant to be."

"For a fact-driven private investigator, you sure are being philosophical."

He laughed quietly. "Relax. Enjoy yourself. This is a once-in-a-lifetime opportunity."

She glanced around the room. "You're right about that much. Thank goodness."

"Stay in touch."

"Believe me, I will."

She snapped the phone shut then slid it into the charger base. What now? She was too keyed up to sleep. She hadn't brought any books. The magazines she'd bought at the airport she'd read on the plane. She didn't think the Moodys or her new boss would appreciate her playing the piano this late, especially given how rusty her skills were. She hadn't played in over a year.

There was only a shower stall in the bathroom, so she couldn't even take a hot bath to help her sleep.

Finally she decided she might as well go to bed, which she found cozy and warm. She closed her eyes…

Julianne stretched as she awoke the next morning, surprised she'd slept until almost seven o'clock. She strolled to the window to get a look at the land in daylight, and found the landscape harshly beautiful, rocky yet dotted with evergreen trees.

Wanting to make a good impression on her new boss, she took the time to straighten her hair with her flatiron, although the humidity would tighten her curls within a couple of hours. She donned dressy black pants and a hunter-green sweater.

She headed down the stairs, ate breakfast alone in the kitchen, then waited for instructions. When none came, she decided to go for a walk. Shoving her hands into her coat pockets, she strained against a surprisingly strong wind. She returned to the castle, offered to help with the housework, was refused, then went for another walk in a different direction, turning back when the castle was almost out of sight.

After dinner, she found sheet music in the piano bench and played for a while. From her room later she saw the man and his dogs on the bluff again and wondered why she hadn't seen the dogs during her walks.

Four days later nothing had changed, except the

previous night when a helicopter had landed nearby. From her window she'd searched for signs of people, but no one approached, either by car or on foot, but later she thought she heard someone crying. The keening sound sent chills through her, then the noise stopped, suddenly, eerily.

Once a day she asked Mrs. Moody when she would meet Mr. Keller and was told, "When he chooses," in a matter-of-fact but also condescending tone.

Quickly Julianne reached the end of her patience and called Jamey. "I'm dying of boredom," she blurted as soon as he picked up the phone. "I miss my mochas. Get me out of here."

"Better than dying of something else."

"Oh, come on, Jamey. I'm not in danger of losing my life, just my independence. And maybe I'd be harassed a little. That's probably more tolerable than Mr. Keller's treatment of me, which is beyond rude. I might as well be in prison." She explained to Jamey that he hadn't so much as introduced himself.

"What about the work he gives you?"

"Not only have I not been given a task to perform, I haven't even seen him. Can you make arrangements for me to go someplace where I can have a life?"

"Let me see what I can do."

"If you don't, I'll find a way myself. I swear." At least now she had ID with her new name. It would make getting another job easier.

Since she hadn't been given permission to use the computer, she hand wrote a letter of resignation to her elusive boss after she hung up with Jamey. At dinnertime, she carried the folded paper with her, intending to give it to Mr. Moody.

"Dinner will be served in the dining room tonight," Mrs. Moody said when Julianne reached the kitchen.

Since she had stopped asking for a reason why things were done the way they were, she went to the dining room without question and was surprised to see two place settings, one at the head of the table, and one next to it.

Company at last. She tucked her letter behind a bowl of shells when she heard footsteps, a steady pace along the hall of the second floor above her, down the long staircase, then the downstairs hallway. A man came through the door. It couldn't be Zach Keller—this man was too young, only about thirty. And he wasn't the dark man who walked the bluff at night, because this one had golden blond hair and bright blue eyes. He extended his hand.

"I'm Zach Keller. Welcome to the Spirit Inn."

Two

Zach watched Julianne's expression transform from surprised to...mutinous? Her crossed arms indicated the latter. Her sweet, citrusy perfume distracted him, reminded him of something. Someone?

"I'm sorry I didn't introduce myself until now," he said.

"Are you?"

He wasn't used to anyone questioning his actions. He could and often did sidestep answering a question, but whatever words came out of his mouth were the absolute truth. Most of the time, he qualified mentally.

"It was rude of me," he said, not rising to her bait. Her stunning hazel eyes didn't flicker. She kept herself so still, her blond curls didn't move but rested against her shoulders. She clamped her mouth shut.

He decided to wait her out, which gave him a moment to recall why her perfume jarred him. Last week, after

Mrs. Moody had unpacked the boxes sent ahead by Julianne, he'd climbed the tower stairs and searched through what she'd sent, trying to get a handle on what she was like, this person who was so important to Jamey. He'd fingered the garments hung in the wardrobe and folded neatly in the dresser drawers, the distinctively lemon fragrance lingering subtly in the fabric and less subtly in his mind.

He'd pictured the body that fit the brightly colored clothing—the impractical abbreviated T-shirts, skirts and shorts; the neon-green bikini bathing suit, and the flimsy lingerie, a lacy rainbow of color that he'd resisted touching. An image of Julianne had formed in his mind—shapely, womanly. Mouthwatering.

Zach often endured long periods of celibacy by choice, this latest bout hitting the seven-month mark. But he'd always been capable of denying his needs, and he didn't expect this time to be any different, even though in person she was even more tempting, her body even more curvy.

"Obviously it took a phone call from Jamey to force you to meet me," she said at last, breaking the increasingly uncomfortable silence. "I feel so welcome."

It didn't matter to him whether she felt welcome. He hadn't wanted her here, had taken her in because for thirteen years he'd owed Jamey a favor, one Jamey hadn't called in until now. "I haven't spoken with him," he said honestly.

She frowned. "Then why are you here?"

"Because it was time. Past time."

She looked him up and down. "I expected an older man."

"I'm sorry to disappoint you."

"I'm not disappointed. I meant, I just figured you were old, since you take naps in the afternoon."

"Sometimes I'm up all night. When that happens, I sleep during the day."

"What do you do?"

"I don't discuss my work."

Judging by her expression, he'd just lost more points. Tough. He would keep his word by giving her a safe haven until her brother's trial was over, even if it meant locking her in a tower.

"You don't discuss your inn?" she asked, challenge in her voice, as if she'd figured out the Spirit Inn didn't really cater to vacationers. "Then how am I supposed to work for you?"

"You will have tasks." He didn't like how she drilled him with her gaze, as if she could see inside his head, but he maintained eye contact.

"Will these tasks have anything to do with the helicopter that arrived last night and left this morning?"

He'd wondered if the sound had awakened her.

"I guess the answer to that is no," she said finally. "I have something for you." She grabbed a folded sheet of paper from behind a large glass bowl on the sideboard.

When she reached, he wondered if she wore something red and lacy under her sweater and jeans…

Her hands shook as she handed him the paper. Zach noticed her cheeks were pink, but he didn't know her well enough to know if it was because of makeup or because she was blushing. Had she caught him admiring her body when she'd turned away?

He read the note, her letter of…resignation, for lack of a better word. Then he folded it and passed it back to her. She crossed her arms again, not accepting the paper.

"You'll stay," he said calmly, tucking the note in his back pocket.

Her brows lifted. "You can't make me."

"I promised Jamey I would look out for you. I don't break promises."

"Jamey is going to find me another position. I'll box up my clothing. I would appreciate it if you could send them to me when I'm settled somewhere else."

"No." He was surprised at her stubbornness. Jamey had told him that Julianne was sweet, a little naive and honorable. Zach would make up his own mind about that. All he knew at this point was that she was more assertive than he'd been led to believe. "I realize that you're lacking the normal amenities and companionship you're accustomed to, but my understanding is that you won't be here for too long."

"I'm not some pampered princess, Mr. Keller. I just want to be useful and to stay busy. I thought I was here to help you, but you've totally ignored me."

"Call me Zach. And that will change now," he said, ending the discussion as Mrs. Moody arrived with the first course. "Please, have a seat, Julianne."

After a moment, she sat. She snapped open her napkin and laid it in her lap, her irritation still obvious, but she also thanked Mrs. Moody and smiled at her, indicating good manners.

Minutes ticked by in long, tense silence, except for the crunch of lettuce. He would've put on some music if he'd anticipated the awkwardness of eating in a total absence of conversation. To turn on the stereo now would be a triumph for her. He couldn't let her get the upper hand.

"I've enjoyed hearing you play the piano," he said after Mrs. Moody exchanged the salad plates for the main course of grilled halibut, rice pilaf and steamed zucchini and carrots—simple food prepared exceptionally well.

"Thank you."

More silence. At first her loftiness amused him. Even though she'd said she wasn't pampered, he knew she must have been indulged for most of her life, first as the daughter, then sister, of a crime boss. She'd likely been sheltered, as would've been necessary. Zach understood this was a transitional time for her. But enough was enough. He set down his fork.

"I acknowledged that you are a fish out of water here, Ms. Johnson. I have apologized for not greeting you sooner. I would appreciate it if you would accept my apology and let us be civil for as long as you're here. That would include dinner conversation."

She also set down her fork, as if in meeting a challenge to a duel. Her expression was one of surprise. "*I* am apparently not allowed to ask questions. If you have questions of me, please feel free to ask them."

Direct hit. He basically *had* told her she couldn't question him, although he'd meant only about his work, not life in general. Politics. Religion.

Sex.

All hot topics, ones he didn't explore with casual acquaintances, no matter how much the mere touch of her clothing and scent of her perfume—without even having met the person—had turned him on. Embarrassingly so.

In a way, she looked like the stereotypical surfer girl. Her hair shimmered in the candlelight, the curls springy and touchable. Her skin looked healthy and tanned. He pictured her in the green bikini he'd rubbed between his fingers. Her breasts would be spilling out of the top, her rear covered but also revealed. She wasn't a size-four waif but a size-twelve handful of pure woman, and shorter than his five-foot-eleven by about eight inches. He admired the disbursement of pounds on her voluptuous frame.

"No questions?" she challenged. "My life is an open book."

Do you have a tan line from that bikini?

"I understand you grew up in Southern California. How'd you end up in San Francisco?" he asked instead.

"My brother sent me there to spy on someone." She took a bite of halibut and smiled at him.

"And did you?"

She nodded.

"Why?"

"Because I wanted something from him. It was a trade."

He waited a few seconds. "Not going to say what it was?"

"No."

"Must've been important."

"Very." She continued to eat.

He almost smiled. Almost. She was having fun at his expense. He liked that she surprised him. "What will you do when your brother's trial is over?"

"I have a plan."

"You're enjoying this, aren't you?"

She took a sip of water, holding his gaze over the edge of the goblet. "Enjoying what?"

"Baiting me."

"Is that what I'm doing?" Her tone was all innocence.

He didn't feel it necessary to answer her obviously rhetorical question.

"Why are so many rooms off-limits to me?" she asked.

"Which ones are you talking about?"

"Your *special* room. The other tower room. The guest rooms."

"You're allowed in the guest rooms. Who said you weren't?"

"Mr. Moody said the only room I could enter on the second floor was my office, which I, of course, have not entered, since I've had no work assigned to me. I would at least like to use the computer to check my e-mail."

"I'll take you up there after dinner. Anything else?"

"You didn't answer my question."

She wasn't easily distracted or deterred. "My 'special' room, as you call it, is just that. You will not be allowed entry. The other tower room is also off-limits. You may go anywhere else in the castle."

"Except your bedroom."

"Yes." *Maybe.* A few choice curses blared in his head at the wayward thought. He scooped up his wineglass and took a quick sip. He'd never had a woman in his bed here. Yet the picture of Julianne's hair spread out on his pillow, the thought of that lush body stretched out on his sheets…

"And you won't enter my tower room," she said.

"Of course not."

"Of course not," she repeated sweetly, her eyes sparkling, as if she were reading his mind, knowing he was more than a little attracted to her. "Good to know. But what about the other tower room? What's the big secret there?"

"Elspeth prefers it be locked."

"Elspeth?"

"The ghost. Mr. Moody told you about her, didn't he?" He watched her eyes open wide. "Obviously not."

"You have a ghost? Seriously?"

"For more than a century, apparently. Angus McMahon's daughter, who died at thirteen."

"From what?"

"Murder most likely, for her to still be unsettled after all this time." He could tell that Julianne was trying hard not to believe him.

"You…see her?" she asked.

"We hear her."

She looked toward the ceiling, then she smiled, tentatively. "You're kidding."

"You'll see."

Mrs. Moody returned, took away their empty plates and left apple pie á la mode and coffee—which meant he and Julianne had more time to fill.

"It's you I've seen walking on the bluff at night, right?" she asked when the coffee was served and Mrs. Moody left. "With two dogs?"

"Yes." He knew she'd been watching, had sensed it even when her window was dark.

"What breed are they?"

"Bullmastiff."

"Are they guard dogs? They're very friendly with you and playful with each other."

"True to the breed, they're fearless and confident, yet also docile. Good companions and protectors."

"And you're very, very good at not answering questions." She raised her coffee cup to him.

"If I'd wanted a lap dog I would've chosen a toy poodle."

She laughed. The sound filled the room with such…joy. There hadn't been much of that in this place. Elation. Relief. Desolation and grief, too. Plenty of that. But not the joyful noise of much laughter. The sound rooted him in his chair.

"Can't say I can picture you with a poodle in your lap," she said, still grinning. "Maybe I could join you in your walk one night? I'd love to see the island in the dark, and to meet your dogs."

"Of course."

"Tonight?"

"If you wish."

Her lips curved upward. "I wish."

For a few seconds, humor fled her eyes, replaced by...he wasn't sure what. Something different, anyway. Hot. Startling. He drew a long, slow breath as they focused on each other. She started to reach a hand toward him, then didn't, looking flustered as she pulled back, the mood cooling.

He was glad the crisis had passed. She would tell Jamey not to find her another position elsewhere, Zach could fulfill his promise, and all would be right in the world again. "After dinner you can check your e-mail while I make a couple of calls, then we'll go for a walk."

"Thank you."

Ahh, much better, indeed. She *was* the naive and sweet young woman that Jamey had labeled her.

She would be easy to manage, after all.

Three

"It's a mild night," Zach commented as they left the castle. "Warm. Considering it's almost December," he added.

Julianne was disappointed at the lack of wind. Because of it Zach wore a light jacket, not the romantic-looking long coat she'd seen him in for the past few nights. He'd made an imposing figure in stark silhouette. His hair, just slightly darker than hers, and long enough to brush his shoulders, had been tossed around by the wind.

She realized she'd created an image of him in her head since she'd arrived, an image that was not entirely accurate. He *was* guarded, cool and private, but he was young, broodingly handsome—his hair waving softly now—and well-spoken. His hermit life hadn't limited his life skills or conversational abilities.

He fascinated her.

And he was also intrigued by her, she thought. She'd

never felt so thoroughly examined, yet with few blatant looks—just the time she'd turned around and caught him eyeing her rear. Whatever he did for a living must include studying people surreptitiously. Had he noticed her attraction to him? It had caught her by surprise, the pull she'd felt, the need to touch him.

Why? Because he was different? Challenging? Commanding? She'd found it arousing arguing with him, keeping up with him.

She'd been attracted to other men, but not like this. Not this sudden, overwhelming pull. And even though he'd made peace with her so that she would stay on, she recognized that Zach represented danger in a way her family's business never had.

Growing up as she had, she was accustomed to men not talking about their work, but it was also something she didn't want to live with again. Too many secrets led to lies, which ultimately led to hurt.

He could easily ruin her plans, turn her life upside down, take something from her she'd never given to anyone else. And for what? A moment of pleasure? She couldn't let that happen. Not now. Not when she stood at freedom's gate at long last. But she hadn't been in this position before, of wanting something, someone, she shouldn't want.

"You're very quiet," he said as they hiked a trail that he must have known by rote, because she saw no path of any kind. They emerged from the trees onto the cleared land up high.

"It's beautiful," she replied, hoping he bought that, although there was enough truth in her words that he should believe her. "And…majestic. I feel like I shouldn't talk."

"Wait till we're at the top."

The sound of muted thunder reached her, getting louder and closer. She drew a quick breath, tucked her arms close and looked around, seeking the source.

"It's the dogs," Zach said softly. He put a hand on her back then whistled, two short, ear-piercing sounds.

Even as his touch soothed, she jumped.

The bullmastiffs' paws pounded the ground with Richter-scale-measurable force. Then, suddenly, they were there, stopping on a dime, dust shrouding their bodies and rising up, their rear ends wriggling, tails wagging as they bumped affectionately against Zach's legs.

He talked to them, petted their heads and scratched their ears. They whined blissfully. Then he introduced them to her.

"Archibald and Annabelle, otherwise known as Archie and Belle. This is Julianne. Be nice to her."

The dogs nudged her hands. The animals were big, easily over one hundred pounds, and their heads came to her waist. While they didn't give her the same loving greeting, they were friendly.

"How dangerous are they?" she asked.

"My security has never been breached."

She didn't ask the questions that popped into her mind, since she knew he wouldn't answer them, but she was curious. Security for what? What did he do behind that locked door?

"Except for your ghost," she pointed out. "I haven't heard any sounds out of the ordinary, by the way. Except I thought I heard someone crying once. The same night that the helicopter landed." She watched him for reaction. Nothing. Not a flicker.

"You must have been dreaming."

"Or it was Elspeth," she said.

"Could be."

She wasn't sure what to make of the ghost story, except he was so serious.

Chills danced down her spine. She decided to change the subject. "Why do you call the Moodys Mr. and Mrs.?"

"What should I call them?"

"They're employees. I would think you would call them by their first names. We're not a formal society anymore."

"It's a sign of my respect for them."

She waited but he added nothing. The dogs started prancing.

"Go," he said to them, and they took off, racing across the bluff, then out of sight. "They'll be back. They'll work off some steam first. Here," he said, extending his hand. "This last part is steep."

She was glad she hadn't worn gloves. His larger hand engulfed hers with warmth. She almost floated up the path behind him until they reached a roadblock, a rocky ledge.

"Wait here a sec," he said, then he leaped up the ledge like a surefooted mountain goat. He turned around, held both hands to her and pulled her up, tugging hard, although to his credit, not groaning at her weight.

She found a foothold. Her body shook as she tried to push off with her bottom leg, but finally let him yank her up. She staggered against him from the momentum, and his body turned to steel, keeping them from tumbling. His arms slipped around her. She held her breath, almost put her face against his chest, then he stepped back and released her.

The silence between them filled with the sound of surf hitting rock. He turned away from her and walked ahead, expecting her to follow, she supposed. Within a few feet she saw the horizon and the lights of the distant island she'd seen during her previous walks. Then she looked down. Her stomach did a somersault at the steep, staggering distance between her and the water, and the long, craggy drop that made her throat close. When she could focus, she saw the white foam of the waves crashing.

"Awesome," she whispered, her body still humming from his touch, but her heart pounding at the vista before her.

"Not a sight a city girl sees very often."

"No, never. I've been to grunion runs at night at the beach, but that's on shore, not a cliff. This is kind of scary. But exhilarating, too." Which pretty much defined her reaction to *him*, as well.

The thunder of paws sounded again. Zach took her by the arm and moved her back from the edge.

"Would the dogs knock me off?" she asked.

"Not on purpose."

"Well, I didn't mean it that way." She saw them running straight at them.

"They can get rambunctious. I just want you in a safer spot."

"If I'm alone here, should I stay away from the edge?"

"That's the safest course, dogs or not."

Archie and Belle came to a stop. Zach talked to them as people often talk to dogs, some words, some nonsense, his tone encouraging.

You would make a good father. The words lit up in her mind, their truth accepted instantly. She'd never thought that about anyone else. Well, maybe Jamey, but no man who'd interested her romantically. Zach parented his dogs with affection and discipline, like a good father would.

She almost groaned. Like she needed something else to like about him.

"Ready to go back?" he asked.

No, but it was probably wise to do so. "Sure. Thank you for bringing me. It's amazing."

He hopped down the ledge, landing with a quiet thud. "Sit down. You can slide a little, then I'll catch you."

Dirt clods loosened beneath her rear as she slid, her toes seeking a landing. His hands slid under her arms, slowing her descent. Distracted by his touch, she was barely aware when she hit ground. Her jacket was down-filled, warm but not too thick. Her breasts were too substantial for him to avoid touching their sides with his arms.

He didn't let her go.

After a few seconds, she lifted her face and locked gazes. His hands didn't move, yet she felt touched all over. Her nipples drew tight. She went up on tiptoe.

He jerked his head back. "This is a bad idea," he said, stepping away.

"Oh, yeah. Right. Bad. Definitely bad." She brushed the seat of her pants, looking at the ground, knowing her face would be flushed. "I was just…Well, anyway."

He walked away.

She followed. They hiked in silence. He didn't hurry, so she had no trouble keeping up, although she wished she'd brought a flashlight. Without him holding her hand, she felt unstable and unsure. She would have to come back on her own in the daylight and get accustomed to the land. She didn't like not being in control, had only recently felt as if she'd finally found her direction in life. This was not a good way to keep moving forward.

They reached the castle.

"Are you going to watch television?" he asked.

"What time is it?"

"Nine."

"Yes. For a while. How about you?"

"I'm going to work." He walked ahead of her until they reached the media room. "I'll see you in the morning, Julianne. I'm glad we finally met."

Had that been just a few hours ago? "Thanks again."

"Sure."

"Oh, Zach. Just one question?"

He cocked his head.

"I'm curious why Elspeth's room is locked. My impression is that ghosts can vaporize and travel wherever they want to." She worked hard to keep innocence in her voice.

"Elspeth prefers it."

"She said so?" Julianne asked, but he just slid his key in the lock then disappeared into his hidey-hole. She smiled. There was no ghost. He liked to perpetuate a myth, when convenient.

She slid a DVD into the player, *The Ghost and Mrs. Muir*, and settled in. She listened for Zach, but he didn't emerge by the time the movie ended and she returned the movie to its box. She considered the exquisite black-and-white film an incredible romance, even though the fiery, sea-captain ghost and the beautiful widow Mrs. Muir couldn't touch or kiss. The seaside house and ocean made Julianne feel even more connected to the film.

In a thoughtful mood, she turned off the television to go to her room. A slight sound stopped her. She stood still, listened hard. Footsteps from above, near—or from—Elspeth's tower room.

"Ridiculous," Julianne muttered. "It's two floors up."

Something heavy fell to the floor, the sound muted as if by a rug. Silence again.

Julianne waited a few seconds then hurried out of the room, through the dining room and kitchen then up her stairs. She shut her door soundly then laughed at herself. Zach had planted the seed of curiosity tonight. Ghosts. Ha!

Still, she didn't take much time to get ready for bed, then pulled the covers up to her chin and stared into the darkness for at least an hour. Just as she finally drifted toward sleep she heard a helicopter again. She threw back the covers and raced to the window in time to see lights from the chopper as it landed quite a distance away.

She saw Zach leave the house and jog into the night, disappearing. She waited and waited and waited. If he returned, it wasn't via the same path. Vague sounds reached her from somewhere within the castle, but it was like an echo chamber, bouncing sound without clarity.

What do you do, Zachary Keller? Are you a smuggler? Contraband of some sort? Illegal substances? People?

Her imagination was working overtime and she was running on empty, tired and yet keyed up. She was tempted to creep down the stairs, but finally decided against it. She wasn't going to cause problems, wanted nothing to interfere with her plans. If they left her alone, she would give them—although she had no idea who "them" might be—their privacy, too.

Her decision made, she went back to bed, knowing she was fooling herself. More than anything she wanted to know what was going on.

Even if it involved ghosts.

Four

Mr. Moody took Julianne to her new office the next morning and explained the job she was to do, entering numbers in a spreadsheet program, tedious work since she couldn't relate them to anything, just numbers and geographical locations without particular meaning to her.

After she'd been working for a while someone came through the open doorway behind her. She'd expected Zach, but it was Mrs. Moody, carrying a mug of something steaming.

"I thought you could use a break," she said.

The rapturous scent of coffee and chocolate reached her nose. Heaven had been brought to her.

"I hope you like mochas," Mrs. Moody said.

"I love them. How did you know?"

"I watch television, too." She offered a hint of a smile. "I know you young people like your fancy coffees."

"I thought maybe you were a mind reader." Julianne took a sip and sighed. "Perfect."

"Let me know whenever you want one." She left soundlessly, not even a disturbance of the air. Like a ghost.

Julianne stopped working to enjoy the hot drink, then proofread her entries, double-checking their accuracy. By noon she was done.

She hadn't seen Zach at breakfast, nor had she heard the helicopter leave, but she'd slept soundly when she'd finally gotten to sleep, so maybe she'd just missed it. She'd hoped to get a daytime glimpse of him. She wasn't aware of any visitors in the castle, either.

After lunch with the Moodys, the afternoon loomed large. She asked if she could go into town, a word she used tongue-in-cheek, since she knew there wasn't much of a town, but maybe she could find some magazines or books to help her pass the time.

She'd accepted that she would stay on the Prom until allowed to leave. She'd called Jamey and told him to forget about finding her another job, and, while he was surprised, he was glad she'd "come to her senses."

She couldn't tell him the reason for her about-face was Zach, because Jamey would probably have something to say about that, words she undoubtedly should hear but didn't want to.

Julianne wasn't used to going it alone. She had close girlfriends whom she was advised not to contact until the whole mess with her brother was over. She couldn't confide in or even just chitchat with the reticent Mrs. Moody. And the consequence of that was that, left to her own devices, Julianne had let her imagination run so wild she'd almost believed the house was haunted. She'd heard nothing, seen nothing, yet she found herself looking and listening. Crazy.

So, she asked to go to town and the answer that came back from Zach via Mr. Moody was yes. She could even take the Jeep. She hesitated then, wondering if Zach wanted her out of the way for some reason.

Still, it was an opportunity to do something new, so she went. Since there was only one main road, she couldn't get lost. Within minutes she pulled up in front of a wooden, two-story building, a hand-carved sign hanging from the porch roof that said, If You're Desperate.

It made her laugh.

Julianne climbed two sturdy stairs, walked across a five-foot-wide porch and entered through the front door. A bell sounded overhead, not a soft tinkling alert, but loud enough to call cows home. Two men and a woman looked her over from their seats at a wood plank table. Coffee mugs and empty paper plates holding wadded-up napkins sat in front of them.

The woman pushed herself up. "I'm Lil," she said, extending her hand. She was about forty years old, had graying, long black hair and wore no makeup, nor did she need it. Her skin glowed. "You must be Julianne."

"My reputation precedes me?" she asked, a little startled then reasoning that Mr. Moody must have called ahead.

"Something like that. My cohorts are Reb and Misery."

The men nodded in greeting. Misery was a tall, skinny African American who looked to be in his thirties, and sixtyish Reb probably hadn't shaved or cut his hair in twenty years, his beard and hair like a furry white blanket.

Like characters out of a story, Julianne thought, enjoying them. She rubbed her hands together. "I came for the action."

Reb laughed, knocking his hand against Misery's arm from across the table.

"Can I get you something?" Lil asked. "Got soda and coffee, but nothing designer or frilly. You have your choice of two sandwiches—tuna salad and tuna melt. No salads. Brownies, though."

"I'd love a brownie and coffee, thank you."

"We serve the high-octane, just so you know."

"Strong's good," Julianne said, taking a seat at the picnic table next to Misery.

"So, you're from Cal-i-for-ni-a," he drawled.

How did he know that? "I am."

"You're one of those surfer girls?"

"I tried it once."

"Once? You give up that easy?"

"I ended up in the E.R. with a concussion. Once was enough."

Reb chuckled. "It's a smart girl who learns a lesson."

"Thank you." She smiled at Lil when she placed the coffee and brownie in front of her then took a seat across from Julianne.

"What do you think of the island of the damned?" Lil asked.

Julianne relaxed, her hands cupping the mug. "Is that what you locals call it? I think it's majestic, but I haven't seen much of it." She glanced around the room, which reminded her of a movie set. Nothing was displayed with designer flair, but the shelves and stacks were dust free, if jammed with everything from razors to toilet plungers, canned beans to bottled water. "I take it people do their grocery shopping elsewhere."

"Orcas Island," Lil said. "A quick boat ride."

In otherwise empty spaces on the walls were pen-and-ink drawings of the island, including the store. They had price stickers attached, but she couldn't read them from where she sat. "Is Orcas the island I can see from the castle?"

"Sure is."

She was aware of her companions' restrained curiosity and decided to open up a little, thinking it might garner some information. "I'm working at the Spirit Inn." She took a bite of the brownie, deep, dark, chocolaty rich and packed with walnuts. Bliss.

"We heard that. How're you liking it?"

"It's a little spooky," she said with a shrug. "Ghosts, you know."

Reb nodded his head thoughtfully.

"Any kind of industry here other than tourist?" Julianne asked.

"Nope." Lil pointed out the window. "There's a day-camp area where people come by boat in the good months. They fish a little. Hike a little. Have a picnic. Then off they go at the end of the day. It's regulars, mostly. We don't have much of interest to draw folks."

"Are there ever any guests at the inn?" There, see? She dropped that question right into the conversation. Julianne was proud of herself.

No one even fidgeted. "This isn't tourist season," Lil said.

Again, not an answer. What about when it *is* tourist season? Julianne wanted to shout. "I guess I won't be around long enough to find out for myself," she said. "I'll be gone before too long."

"We heard that, too."

Julianne got a kick out of that comment. Like any small town, word traveled. She was just surprised that Zach was talking about her. Or maybe he wasn't. Maybe he'd planted just enough information to deflect curiosity. Still, the three people at the table seemed to protect his privacy. Why? How much did they know about what he did? And why wasn't she allowed to know?

"I've heard a helicopter a couple of times," she offered as bait.

Silence hovered for several long seconds, then Misery said, "Julianne, if you're looking for information on your boss, you'd best be asking him. We don't interfere in each others' lives around here. And we safeguard our own. You're an outsider. A pretty one, and one with spunk, I can tell, but you don't belong."

She decided if she wanted to keep coming to If You're Desperate for conversation and a change of pace, she'd better play the game differently. "Lil, this is the best brownie I've ever eaten."

"It's the weather."

"Huh?"

"Something about the weather on this island makes 'em so good. Like San Francisco is good for sourdough. I tried to make these elsewhere, but…" She shrugged.

Julianne finished her brownie, picked up her mug and wandered over to examine one of the drawings. It was like looking through her tower window. She glanced at the price—one hundred dollars. The cost was out of place in the tiny store in the middle of nowhere, which made Julianne more curious. She could just make out a signature in the lower right corner, an *H* followed by a half-inch wavy line leading into another *H,* although both *H*s were stylized so they might have been *K*s or *R*s. *K* and *R?* Keller? No, she was pretty sure they were *H*s.

"A local artist?" she asked.

"We have a few," Lil said. "Some pretty famous ones."

"But you respect their privacy."

Lil smiled. "Lots of little artist colonies here and about. Those creative types seem to fancy their space."

"And don't fancy other people."

"Some of 'em. Strange bunch."

Misery stood. "Time for me to get a move on. Nice meeting you, Julianne. Come back and visit."

She shook his hand, then Reb joined him. They left together.

Alone with Lil, Julianne wondered how the woman made enough money to survive. Maybe she didn't. Maybe she didn't need to. Strong personal reasons must have driven the residents here, stronger than making money in the usual ways.

"Enjoying your time here on the Prom?" Lil asked.

"I'd like to be busier, but yes, I am."

"If you're considering taking a drive after you leave here, you can keep going around the bend. Stick to the road and don't wander off onto private property."

"Are there signs posted?"

"If it's not on the beaten path, it's private."

All these cautions. It was like a soap opera and mystery all together. "It must take a special kind of person to live like this."

"That's a matter of opinion, I guess."

Julianne decided she'd worn out her welcome. No one wanted to give her answers, and their doubts or concerns about her would not go away with one conversation. "How much do I owe you?" she asked Lil.

"First time's on the house."

Julianne shook her hand. "I enjoyed meeting you."

"Gotta say, you aren't what I expected," Lil said as they walked to the door.

"I don't suppose you're going to expand on that comment?"

"Already got me figured out, do you, Julianne?"

"Rome wasn't built in a day, as they say."

"Nope. It sure wasn't. You come back."

"I will. Thanks."

She took Lil's advice and drove as far as she could on the main road, stopping a couple of times to admire the view. She saw two, possibly three, other islands in the distance and wondered about them. She knew that one hundred and seventy islands made up what was called the San Juans, but few of them were very touristy or had good-size populations. She wondered if Mr. Moody would take her to a couple of them by boat so that she could explore. They'd entered the rainy season, though, so maybe it wouldn't be an easy thing to do.

She spotted the day-camp area on her way back to the castle and decided the island couldn't possibly call it a tourist trade. Very few people must visit.

As she pulled up beside the castle, Zach came out of the house. In the light of day he looked more like the Brawny guy, a kind of lumberjack look that suited him— plaid flannel shirt with sleeves rolled to just below his elbows. Sturdy jeans. Boots. His blond hair looked like it'd been raked with his fingers to comb it, the ends touching the back of his collar. He stood, feet planted, thighs filling the denim fabric, from all that hiking, she supposed. His arms hung loosely by his sides, so she couldn't determine from his body language whether he was irritated. If he'd crossed his arms she would know how to approach him.

So she just said hi.

"Have fun?" he asked.

"I did. Met a few of your friends."

"Lil, Reb and Misery."

So…he was letting her know that nothing happened that he didn't hear about.

"An interesting bunch." She rested a hip against the side of the Jeep. "Keep their own counsel well."

He nodded.

She realized she'd forgotten to look for books or magazines. "Do you have another job for me?"

"Not at the moment. I'm considering giving you a project. Need to think about how it should be done."

The sun broke through a cloud. Warmth infused her. She closed her eyes and enjoyed it. "I saw some artwork," she said, keeping her eyes closed. "Pen-and-ink drawings of the island, particularly views from here." She remembered the possibility of the letters being *K* and *R*. "Are you the artist?"

"I only moved here three years ago."

She opened her eyes. He'd moved here three years ago. So what? The drawings could've been done yesterday, for all she knew. Or twenty years ago. "Meaning, they were done before you bought the place?"

"I'm saying that a lot of people have stayed here."

"There's a signature, and a price tag of a hundred dollars. That's pretty steep for an amateur artist." She would try an Internet search. At least it would give her something to do.

"I agree."

Again an answer but not an answer. He was frustratingly

good at deflection. She slipped out of her jacket as the clouds opened up further and let more sun through. Zach's gaze touched her almost physically.

"Your clothes aren't really suited to winter here," he commented, his tone of voice casual but his inspection of her not casual at all. She felt…thoroughly examined.

"I'd go shopping, but…"

"Mr. Moody would take you to Orcas, if you want. Or into Anacordes on the mainland. You're not a prisoner, Julianne. You're being protected. They are entirely different things." He came closer, until he could lean against the car with her and enjoy the sun on his face, too.

"Where are you from?" she asked, studying him, enjoying looking at him.

"Near San Francisco."

"How old are you?"

"Thirty."

"Are you happy living in this kind of isolation?" She couldn't understand anyone voluntarily living so far from civilization—from shopping.

"I chose to."

"That's not an answer, Zach." She waited a few beats. "Do you leave the island?"

"Regularly."

"Where do you go?"

"All over. No place in particular."

"Do you have a family?"

"Everyone has a family."

She blew out a breath. "A family you see? Communicate with? Like?"

"Yes."

That surprised her. She'd pegged him as a loner.

"How about you, Julianne? Aside from your brother, do you have family?"

She hesitated, not really wanting to think about it. But fair was fair. He'd answered her question, sort of. "My dad died ten years ago. I have uncles and cousins. I'm not close to them."

"Your mom?"

She looked away sharply. "Left us when I was little."

"Abandoned you?"

He'd softened his tone with kindness, which surprised her, and drew her gaze back to his.

"Yes," she said, the word coming out shaky. "I haven't seen or heard from her in twenty years. It was her way of getting out from the family business. If she'd taken my brother and me along, they would've tracked her down no matter what. So she left. Disappeared. Never to be heard from again." The pain of knowing her mother had given her up so selfishly never left her. "I figured Jamey filled you in on my history."

"A little. He said your brother was going to trial, and you needed a place to stay, and that anything else I needed to know you would tell me."

Julianne didn't know whether she would've preferred Jamey have told Zach about her past. Saying it out loud sounded harsh, even though she'd been innocent herself— at least of committing a crime.

"I'd be interested in knowing," he said, "whenever you'd like to talk about it."

"There's a lot I'd be interested in knowing about you, too." She wanted the conversation to end, so she smiled benignly at him. "We could trade, fact for fact."

"So you're a deal maker."

"I'm bored. And I'm curious."

"It's for your sake, not mine, that I can't share what I do. Trust me. It's better this way."

"You know, I've heard that 'trust me' thing most of my life. That other people know what's best for me," she said, annoyed. "I decided not to take it at face value anymore. People earn trust. And I do know what's best for myself."

"Fair enough."

That let the wind out of her sails. She'd wanted a little debate, some emotion, something energizing. He'd stopped the potential for any of that.

"You could've argued the point just a little," she muttered.

"I know."

Irritated, she gave him a little shove, but smiled at him. He didn't smile. He simply looked at her, his gaze intense and heated. Had she crossed a line, touching him? Some boss/assistant, protector/protectee demarcation visible only in *his* mind?

Or was it desire? Had her touch done that?

She was tired of the games men played. Part of her plan—no, her ultimate dream—had been to find a man who was open and direct and trustworthy, something she'd never really known and desperately wanted. Zach was about as closed and indirect as they came, although probably trustworthy. She didn't think Jamey would've sent her to someone he didn't truly trust.

Still, there was a difference between trusting a person as a person, and a man as a man, one half of a relationship, no matter how fascinating that man was. Some day she hoped she would get to appreciate the difference.

"I would say I should get back to work, but…" She let the sentence drift. "Do you have a library or something?"

"What do you like to read?"

"To be honest, I like magazines." She remembered she was going to research the artist on the Internet. "On second thought, maybe I'll just check my e-mail."

She pushed away from the Jeep. He didn't stop her. "Will you be joining me for dinner?"

"Probably."

"Okay." She felt his gaze on her as she walked away. His silent intensity flattered and aroused her. She wondered how much her hips swayed. Had she changed her stride, wanting to attract him? Probably. Anticipation and need skirmished within her, slowing her down. It felt good. Too good. Freeing.

But not something she dared to dream about. Not yet, anyway. Later, when she was on her own and independent.

That day couldn't come soon enough for her.

Five

Nothing. Julianne found nothing on the Internet about an artist from Promontory Island. How else could she research? Entering the first and last letters of a name was too vague for the search engine to turn up anything but millions of possibilities to wade through. She'd searched specific names like Spirit Inn, and other geographical places nearby, trying to narrow down the numbers, but...nothing. And she assumed there were many artists who lived or had lived on the island, not just the mysterious $H\rule{1cm}{0.4pt}H$, if, in fact, those were the right letters. K and R still might be right, after all.

What could fit? She logged on to a baby-name site and scoured the lists for combinations of H, K and R. Hank. Harper. Heath. Hersh. Hitch. Homer. Hugh. Hutch. She wrinkled her nose. She didn't know why, but she thought the artist was a woman. There was a certain delicacy to the lines.

So...women's names. Hannah. Heather. A short list.

The double-H names, then: Heath, Hersh, Hugh and Hannah. But those were all first names, not last. Too many possibilities for last names.

She drummed her fingers on the mouse pad and frowned at the monitor. If the asking price hadn't been so high, she wouldn't have been so curious. But to charge over twenty dollars for what amounted to a hand-drawn postcard made her wonder.

She really had way too little to do.

She logged off the Internet, played a few hands of solitaire then shut down the computer. Time for dinner. How would their conversation be tonight? Tense? Relaxed? Stilted? Would they begin to share information? Most likely he would draw information out of her, and she would be left empty-handed. She figured he revealed nothing accidentally. But she'd lived for too many years with secretive men not to have figured out when she was being ignored or patronized.

Julianne headed into the dining room then came to a quick stop inside the door. Only one place setting.

Mrs. Moody swept into the room.

"I'll be alone?" Julianne asked.

"Mr. Zach had to leave."

"The island?"

"Yes." She set down the tray, then moved a bowl of beef stew and basket of bread onto the tabletop.

"I didn't hear the helicopter."

"He went by boat."

Julianne mulled that over. She hadn't considered he would travel much by boat, but she should have. "When will he be back?"

"He wasn't sure."

"Tonight?"

"No. Tomorrow afternoon at the earliest. May I get you anything else?"

Answers. "When he's not going to be here for dinner, I'd really prefer to eat with you and Mr. Moody," she said. "I get lonely here all by myself. I'd appreciate your including me at the kitchen table."

"All right."

"And I'd like to be given some tasks to do. I'm not used to sitting on my hands. It's a big house. Surely I could help."

Mrs. Moody nodded. "I'll find something."

"Thank you."

"Enjoy your dinner." She left, as ghostlike as always.

Maybe she wasn't real, Julianne thought, grinning at the fanciful idea. Stir-crazy, that's what she was becoming. And she probably had months more of this ahead of her?

She finished the delicious meal and returned the dishes, then washed them. The piano called her. At least that was something positive. Her skills were sharpening, even if the selection of music was skimpy.

After an hour of playing Brahms and Handel—well out of her comfort zone—she wandered down the hall to the media room, looked behind her, then walked past it to the next door. She wrapped her hand around the doorknob to Zach's locked room, the inner sanctum, the forbidden place. The knob didn't budge.

She almost thumped a fist on the wooden door. *What is in there? Why the big secret?* She couldn't imagine Jamey sending her to someone who was breaking the law, not given her past, so what could it be?

Julianne heard footsteps from upstairs, as she had the other night. Mrs. Moody's steps were too ethereal for them to be hers, yet they also seemed too quiet to belong to Mr. Moody, or any man.

This time the person continued to walk at a steady pace, reaching a spot and turning around, repeating the steps.

Julianne glanced in both directions, listened for any sound indicating the Moodys were nearby, then she crept down the hall and made a right turn toward one of the guest rooms. The sound overhead increased slightly in volume.

She tiptoed the rest of the way, to the bottom of the stairs, toward the other tower room. Louder, heavier footsteps, although not truly loud nor heavy, except in comparison. Someone was in the tower room.

Elspeth?

Julianne laughed nervously, then clamped a hand over her mouth. Perspiration glued her sweater to her body. She tried the door handle. Locked.

As if she would've opened the door and gone up the stairs. Right.

The sounds stopped, then something scraped along the floor. She jumped, pressed her back against the stone wall, cold seeping inside her, slithering through her entire body. Another scrape, then silence. Complete silence.

Outside, the dogs began to howl. Julianne shoved away from the wall, hurried down the hallway, turned and raced past the locked chamber, the media room, the living room. Across the entry, through the dining room, into the kitchen.

She zoomed up her stairwell, and into her room. She shut the door, leaned against it. Okay. O-kay. Her feet slipped out from under her a little. She dug in her toes. Caught her breath. Closed her eyes.

The dogs howled again. She felt her way to the window, knelt on the seat and peered outside. Darkness greeted her, not even silhouettes of trees or rocks, because clouds blocked the moon.

She felt silly at her unexpected shivering. She wanted to go home—or rather to wherever her new home was going to be. She wanted to eat at a Mexican restaurant and taste the salted rim of a limey margarita, to dance at a loud and crowded club, to shop for something frivolous, like long, gaudy earrings and fake-jewel-encrusted sandals.

And this was only day seven.

Mrs. Moody set a can of paste wax and a few rags in Julianne's hands the next morning and pointed her to the living room. Zach had showed her how to put a CD in the stereo in the media room then turn switches to get the music to other rooms, so she piped tunes into the living room while she worked. The Rolling Stones gave her a good beat to polish wood by. Every so often one of the Moodys poked their head in the room. Determined to win them over, she invited them to dance, received a slight smile and shake of the head in response, then off they would go again.

She cherished those small smiles. One of the things she'd realized about herself over the past few months when she'd been a waitress, while also being a spy, was that she accommodated people well because she liked to be liked, although she hadn't been a particularly good waitress. Her distraction level was too high to remember the details that good servers recall and do well.

However, she felt different with Zach. She wanted to push him for details, because she wanted to understand him. And she nudged Mr. and Mrs. Moody because they intrigued her, as well.

After lunch Mr. Moody announced he was taking the boat to the mainland to pick up Zach. Mrs. Moody always took an hour's rest after lunch. Julianne was at loose ends. She'd finished the polishing, had checked her e-mail. Maybe she would take a walk with the dogs.

She went to her room for her jacket, spotted Archie and Belle scampering across the bluff, and wondered again why they'd howled last night—if it was them. She hurried downstairs to catch up with them, then decided to take dog biscuits as a get-to-know-them bribe. As she closed the biscuit tin she heard a thump, not from directly overhead but farther away. The tower room again?

Daytime seemed a better—safer?—time to explore the bumps in the night. She eased down the hallway, stopping out of habit at the locked door. This time the knob turned.

Startled at the door popping open, Julianne went rigid as she contemplated her next move. Mrs. Moody should be in her room for another forty-five minutes or so. Julianne looked both ways then pushed the door open farther with her fingertip. She peered inside.

The large room looked like a command center. Several computers, monitors and printers sat on desks. A white-erase board was filled with the same kind of codes Julianne had been entering in the computer for Zach. Heart pounding, she stepped into the room. Photos were tacked on three walls, people of all ages and race. There didn't seem to be a unifying element tying them together, at least not physically. Straight ahead were just a few photos, thumbtacked to a wall covered in cork. To her right many were on display, maybe a hundred. To her left she counted thirty-two. Broken into categories, she decided, but for what?

She zeroed in on one photo. The woman looked familiar.

Julianne took another step forward, then another, drawing closer. The woman was in her early twenties, and beautiful—

The same scraping sound from overhead jarred her again. Panicked at the thought of being caught, she hurried out of the room and closed the door quietly, her hands—her whole body—shaking. She moved away from the room, but not toward the tower, ducking into the media room instead where she dropped onto a couch and sat quivering.

What was Zach involved in? Did Jamey know?

What could all those photos represent? Who was the woman? Why would she be familiar? Why did a helicopter come and go? Why was he so mysterious?

Why had he said he was keeping her in the dark for her own protection, not his?

Agitated, she decided to go for a walk, not with the dogs, after all, but into town, the distance giving her time to calm down. She almost ran down the road then realized she hadn't left Mrs. Moody a note saying where she'd gone. Although she carried her cell phone, she didn't want to awaken the housekeeper, so she ignored her breach in etiquette and would apologize later.

As Julianne hit the bottom of the hill, a speedboat was headed away from the island. Lil strolled up from the dock, a bag in her hands. She waited for Julianne to join her, then they walked to If You're Desperate together.

"Mail," Lil said, holding up the bag.

"Are you the postmistress here, too?"

"I'm authorized." Lil studied her. "You look like you've seen a ghost."

Julianne laughed, the sound wobbly. "Maybe."

Lil's brows lifted high.

"Just noises. Creaky old castle stuff." She looked away. "Do you believe in ghosts?"

"I haven't had any personal experience."

Everyone shut doors in Julianne's face by not really answering questions. It was frustrating. "How long have you lived here?" she asked Lil as they stepped into the store.

"A couple of years."

Julianne would have expected it to be longer. "Why here?"

"Why not here?" She smiled just a little.

"Do you make a living?"

"As much of one as I need to."

Julianne sighed. "I guess I need to stop asking questions."

"You do seem overly curious."

"I have a naturally curious personality."

Lil laughed. "Yes. Have a seat. Can I get you something?"

She realized the knots had almost loosened in her stomach. "Anything sweet."

"Freshly baked oatmeal-and-chocolate-chip cookies." She slid two on a napkin in front of Julianne. "Was there something in particular you wanted?"

"I was wondering if you carry books or magazines?" She took a bite of cookie and savored it.

"Got a few books but not for sale. More of a lending library. You're welcome to borrow some." Lil pointed to a shelf behind Julianne then opened the bag of mail and started sorting.

"Thanks." She wandered over to look at the titles. Now that she knew she wouldn't get information out of Lil no matter how hard she tried, she wondered what to talk about. "How much rain should I expect during the winter?"

"Enough to keep you housebound quite a bit. You'll probably want to take the boat over and do some shopping for reading material, and anything else that might help keep you occupied."

Out the window Julianne spotted a boat headed to the dock. Zach and Mr. Moody. She could hitch a ride back up the hill with them…

Her heart began to race. Would Zach know what she'd done?

She needed to calm down or he, with his above-average observation skills, would know she was guilty of something.

"Is there mail for Zach?" she asked Lil, figuring if she had something to do, she could stop thinking about what she'd done. "I could take it to him."

Lil grabbed a couple of envelopes. "I'll walk with you."

Zach waved as they approached. He met them halfway as Mr. Moody got into the Jeep and waited.

"I walked down," Julianne said before he asked. She paused, getting caught up in those bright blue eyes keying on her, making her nervous. "I, um, could use a ride back."

"Sure." He studied her in the same way Lil had, then he glanced at the older woman. "How's everything?"

"Good." She passed him the mail. "You?"

"Not bad. Anything new?"

"Nothing," Lil said. "Nothing at all."

Something passed between them, something tangible, like a private code given and received, and an understanding. Julianne felt left out. Did it have something to do with all those photos tacked on the wall in the secret room. Was Lil in on it, too—whatever *it* was?

Julianne stared at the back of Zach's head as they rode to the castle. He held himself stiffly. In profile she saw his jaw clench and release, clench and release. He didn't even seem aware of her, he'd sunk so deeply into himself. An urge to hug him, to comfort him, swept through her. She wanted to reach out and stroke the back of his head, down his neck, across his shoulders.

She wanted to bring him peace.

And she felt overwhelmingly guilty about having gone into his sanctuary, even as she struggled to remember where she'd seen the woman in the photo.

Julianne was not a devious person. She'd always believed herself trustworthy, but entering a room she'd been told specifically to stay out of proved she couldn't be trusted, after all. It shocked her.

After they climbed out of the Jeep, Zach left her without a word. Confused, and a little hurt, she followed but he was already out of sight. She wandered into the living room. On the piano bench was a package, wrapped in brown paper and tied with a string. She looked around. Was it for her?

She untied the string. Inside the bag was a stack of sheet music of all kinds—Disney tunes, country, movie music, rags, old standards. Her eyes stung. She'd broken his trust, and he'd bought her sheet music.

She drew the package against her chest, her heart pitter-patting, warming her. Should she tell him what she'd done? Yes. She needed to be an adult and take responsibility for her actions. After dinner, she decided, when he was well fed and relaxed.

In the meantime she would sort through the music and choose something to practice.

"Julianne."

Zach stood in the doorway.

"Zach!" She hurried toward him. "Thank you so much. You have no idea—"

"Come with me, please."

His expression was one she hadn't seen before, not exactly emotionless, but definitely cool. Distant. She followed him down the hall. He stopped at the door to his secret room, turned the knob and pushed it open, waited for her enter. Her pulse thundered in her ears.

He knew. Somehow he knew.

She made her feet move, and entered the room. He shut the door quietly behind them. Too quietly. Tension filled the air like a living thing. Accusation came from every pair of eyes in every photo on the walls.

"I asked one thing of you, Julianne. One. To stay out of this room. You disobeyed."

"I was going to tell you tonight. I—"

He made a gesture, silencing her.

"Your trespassing has consequences, huge ones. Far reaching." He shoved his hands through his hair. "I can't believe you put me in this spot."

"I don't even know what all this means," she said, sweeping the room with her gaze, again trying to make sense of the photographs. She wondered if he had a camera in the room, if that was how he'd known.

She took a step toward him, then it struck her who the woman was. She sought the photo again. She'd seen the woman on television last month, a kidnap victim who'd been brutally murdered.

She took a few steps back. Fear struck her, lodging her heart in her throat. She shook her head. "I'll…I'll leave the Prom. I'll find my own way." She kept moving toward the door. Where could she go? How could she get off the island?

His eyes narrowed. "You recognize someone on the wall."

"No, I—"

"You do." He moved, blocking her exit. "Who?"

She shook her head again.

"Don't compound the damage you've done with more lies."

She pointed. "Her, all right? *Her.*" She tried to inch her way around him.

"You're afraid of me," he said, as if surprised. As if she had no reason. "You think I had something to do with her kidnapping? Her murder?"

"Did you?"

"No. And you're just going to have to trust me on that."

"How can I?"

"Because I say so."

"Because you say so?" An almost hysterical laugh escaped her, small and shaky. "I'm sorry I violated your trust, but—"

"Sorry? Yes, I'm sure you are, and about to become more so." He put a hand under her chin and lifted her face toward him. "Because now you have to marry me."

Six

Zach at least got some satisfaction in watching her face drain of color.

"No," she said finally.

"Yes. As soon as possible."

"Why?"

"Because a wife can't testify against her husband."

She stared back at him. "I think I need to sit down."

He gestured toward a chair. Damn. Why had she done it? When he'd stepped into the room a few minutes ago he'd smelled her perfume. He was stunned at first, not believing it possible, thinking maybe the scent had drifted from elsewhere, through vents or something. But she wasn't in the house, had been gone for more than an hour. What was in the air was left over, not new. If she hadn't worn a fragrance so distinctive, she would've gotten away with it.

"What do you do?" she said, then hesitated. "Never

mind. I don't want to know what you do. I'll go away. Today. No one will even know I was here."

"Many people already know."

"People who are loyal to you."

She had a point. "Yes, but they chose their situation. You didn't. And you would be the one to be hurt most. I'm protecting *you*, Julianne."

Some fire returned to her. She stood and faced him. "I've been protected my whole life. I have a plan. You are *not* going to interfere in my plan. I can take care of myself."

He shook his head.

She threw up her hands. "Men. You think you're always right. You're not."

"I don't profess to always be right. This time I am, though." Despite the seriousness of the topic he was fascinated by her reaction. Her face was flushed, her fists plunked sassily on her hips, her curls bouncing with every emphatic word.

She closed her eyes and seemed to count to ten. "Look," she began, much more calmly. "I see photographs on the wall and computer equipment. I have no idea what it all means. If anyone asked, that's all I could tell them."

"You recognized Carolyn Keely."

His statement hovered in suspended animation for several long seconds.

"What I do is illegal, Julianne. Almost every day I am committing a crime. But I won't let anything keep me from my job. It's too important." He dismissed her objections with his tone of voice alone. "We'll go to Friday Harbor tomorrow and get the license. Unfortunately there's a three-day waiting period." He crossed his arms. "You can go now."

She moved past him but stopped, her hand on the doorknob. "There has to be another solution."

She left soundlessly, except for the quiet latch of the door. Her distinctive scent lingered, stronger than when he'd first realized she'd been in the room.

He stared at the wall above the computers until the photos blurred. He didn't need to look at them. They were branded in his mind—Theresa Rogers, age twenty-two; Daniel Doty, age eleven, and Jacob Munson, fifteen months.

Zach moved forward, wiggled the tack out of Theresa's picture, then moved it to a different wall. Theresa's terrified expression had haunted Zach for seventeen days. No more, though.

He walked to another wall, his gaze lingering on each photo, one at a time. He knew their vital statistics, could bring up every detail, including Carolyn Keely's. Failures. And even one was too many.

He returned to the wall holding only two photos, Jacob and Daniel. "I'll find you," he said, low and harsh, his obsession acknowledged then ignored as he sat at the computer to record Theresa's information.

At six o'clock he called Mrs. Moody on the intercom and asked her to bring his dinner into his command center, deciding he was in no mood to eat in strained silence or hostility or whatever mood Julianne would be in now.

She could eat alone.

Julianne barely touched her food. She pushed peas and carrots around her plate, stabbed at the perfectly roasted slices of turkey breast, then gave in and ate the mashed potatoes. No feeling of comfort followed. She set her fork on the plate, wishing she could throw it instead, and pushed away from the table.

How had this happened? Punishment was supposed to

fit the crime, but it wouldn't in this case. Okay, so she'd violated his trust. She'd already admitted how wrong she'd been, how shocked she was by the fact she'd done such a thing. But, marriage? For how long?

She considered running away, but had no idea how to get herself off the island without public transportation. She considered telling Jamey he needed to come rescue her. She could go underground for however long was necessary.

And exactly what was it that Zach was afraid would happen? She honestly didn't know what he did, what crime he committed daily, so how could she be a problem?

At least she had three days to change his mind. Or disappear.

Restless, she decided to go for a walk. She wouldn't go far since it was already dark and she wasn't overly familiar with the paths yet, but if she stayed in this house one more minute…

She put her dishes on the dinner tray and carried it out the door then spied Zach, his back to her, turning the corner of the hallway at the exact same time. She set down the tray and hurried to catch up, hoping to present her opening argument against their marrying.

She rounded the corner in time to see him unlock the door to the tower room and disappear inside. After a quick surveillance she tiptoed quickly down the hall, could hear his footsteps as he climbed. A door opened and closed, then voices, low and indistinct, reached her—his and a woman's.

A woman. No ghost. No Elspeth. A woman. Locked in the tower room.

Held prisoner?

Julianne's imagination ran wild. An old castle on an

isolated island. A ghost as a cover story, but a cover for what? A crazy relative in the attic? Why keep the door locked? Obviously someone dangerous. Related to his committing criminal acts?

A knot formed in Julianne's stomach. Zach Keller was a walking secret. How could she continue to stay on, much less marry him?

Marry.

She couldn't do that. She just couldn't, even if it meant putting herself in whatever situation he thought she was in because of what she knew.

The woman's voice went up in decibels, the words still indistinct but she was obviously upset. Zach's voice remained level. A soothing tone. Something hit the wall and then scattered on the floor, startling Julianne so that she banged her head against the wall. Zach said something with a note of finality, then he started down the stairs.

Julianne sped down the hall and around the corner. She zoomed into the dining room, scooped up the tray and headed for the kitchen, her heart thumping, breath hitching.

She knew the exact moment he spotted her, but she kept walking.

"Julianne, wait."

She could obey or defy him. Keep the peace or make him angry. She didn't want him to see her vulnerable or afraid of him, but she was both. So, she ignored him. He followed her into the kitchen.

Before he could speak she set down the tray with a bang and turned on him. "I will not marry you."

"You will." He used a light but matter-of-fact tone.

"Who is locked in the tower?" she blurted out, then clamped her mouth shut as his jaw turned to granite. What had gotten into her? Why was she saying and doing things she'd never believed herself capable of?

"What goes on in this house is none of your business."

"If I'm going to be your wife, I deserve to know what I'm getting into."

"You're going to be my wife in name only."

The attraction she'd felt for him since they'd met had gotten lost in the heat of the day's events. The "in name only" reminded her how one-sided the attraction was, even though she'd thought otherwise. How could she have been wrong about that? And how could she be attracted to a man who kept so many secrets, who wouldn't share his life—who committed crimes?

Been there, done that. Won't live that secretive life again.

She turned her back on him and headed to her room. She'd barely shut the door when it burst open.

He closed in on her. "You brought this on yourself by disobeying my rules. None of this would've happened if you hadn't been nosy and reckless. None of it."

She stood her ground. "I take full responsibility."

"I am not going to spend the next three days arguing with you about the marriage. It's going to happen. Get used to it."

"I'm going to spend the next three days trying to find a way out. Get used to it," she said calmly, as her heart raced. Someone was in the attic. Had to be *locked* in the attic.

Something flickered in his eyes. Respect? Annoyance? It was hard to tell.

"Fair enough," he said finally. "Would you like to go for a walk?"

His abrupt turnaround caught her off guard. "Yes," she answered without thinking. "But I don't want to talk," she added.

His mouth twitched. He must think her a total idiot.

"Fine with me." He grabbed her jacket, holding it for her to put on but not touching her.

Now that she'd set the rules, she had to adhere to them. He seemed amused, which irritated her even more. They climbed the path to the bluff. The dogs came from out of nowhere and she talked to them, played with them. When they took off, she and Zach climbed the rest of the way. He helped her as he had before, but this time his touch took on more significance as she fell against him. And this time when they reached the top, he sat down, as if they had all the time in the world. It would seem petulant if she didn't do the same, so she sat, but a good five feet away from him—which also seemed to amuse him.

It was hard saying nothing. She wanted to ask about the other islands, sneak in a few questions that might help in her quest to leave. After a while the dogs returned. Belle lay beside Zach and put her head in his lap. Archie curled up next to Julianne, his body warm against her hip and thigh.

"They're good dogs," she said, unable to keep quiet a second longer.

Zach gave her a lopsided smile but was gentleman enough not to comment on her breach.

Silence. She squirmed. He obviously wasn't going to make this easy on her. "I never knew guard dogs could be lap dogs, too."

Louder silence. She picked up pebbles and tossed them far in the air, then they dropped to the ocean. The waves hitting rocks below kept a steady rhythm.

"I don't like secrets, Zach."

"Sometimes they're necessary, Julianne."

"Secrets only end up hurting people."

"Some secrets help people."

"Not in my experience."

"Obviously we've had different experiences."

"I'm here because of secrets."

He scanned the horizon. "So am I."

She sighed.

"The marriage won't be forever," he said after a while.

Archie lifted his head as she reacted. "How do you know that? Are you going to quit what you're doing?"

"Never. When it's right we'll dissolve the marriage."

"How long do you think that will be?"

"I don't know."

"Ballpark. A month? A year? Two years? Five?"

"I don't know."

"That doesn't work for me, Zach."

He shrugged, infuriating her.

"Maybe you don't understand what I've gone through all my life," she said. "If you did, I think you'd let me go now and find my own way."

"Why don't you tell me what that means."

If it would help her escape the marriage, she would tell him anything. She relaxed, and Archie settled next to her again. "I've been a pawn all my life. All my life. First my father dictated my every move, chose my friends and activities, then when he died, my brother, Nico, did. I lived in a mansion. For most of my life I thought we were respectable, if a little odd. There were comings and goings, but I learned not to ask questions. I was chauffeured everywhere. You might have thought that was a girl's dream, but I hated it, especially when I was old enough to drive but wasn't allowed to get my license."

"You don't drive?"

"I drove the Jeep, didn't I? I took lessons while I lived in San Francisco, but I haven't driven much. I don't own a car."

"A rarity in California."

"Tell me about it. Since I wasn't physically allowed to attend college, I had to take Internet-only classes."

"What was your brother afraid of?"

"My brother took my dad's lucrative bookie business and turned it into something big. Extortion, money laundering, the works."

"When did you find out?"

She rested her chin on her knees. "I would hear things by accident. Eventually I put two and two together. I was twenty. I wanted to live on my own and go to college like any other girl my age. He refused. I told him he couldn't stop me. But he could. I was a target. He had enemies…" Just the thought of that conversation when he sat her down and told her why she couldn't live independently gave her the shakes. She could be kidnapped—

Like Carolyn Keely. Killed. That truth had never hit her quite so hard before.

"How did you finally get out?"

She sat up, not letting on how shaken she was. "He needed me to spy on someone living in San Francisco, someone I learned after the fact he'd extorted money from well above and beyond what she should've had to pay. I was supposed to get close enough to her that she would confide in me, and I would know if she learned the truth and contacted the police. In exchange, he was going to give me enough money to go away. New ID. Everything. A new life."

"You looked forward to that, I guess."

"I didn't like giving up my friends, but for the chance

to finally live my own life? Yes, I looked forward to it."
Ached for it. It wasn't supposed to be so hard to get to that
point in her life.

"And instead you end up here, isolated."

"And trapped. Yet another man dictating my life."

"You took your own choices away."

Tears burned in her throat. How had her life gotten so
complicated? She'd only wanted her freedom, had only
expected to have to put in a little time and then she would
be on her way.

Now she was at the mercy of a man she didn't trust,
and was ridiculously attracted to. What happened to her
simple plan?

"You're shivering," he said, then stood and offered her
a hand up. Because it suited her, she accepted his help up,
then he didn't let go of her hand.

"I understand how disappointed and angry you are,
Julianne. I will try to make this as easy on you as possible.
But to do that, you have to meet me halfway."

His thumb rubbed the back of her hand, distracting her.
"What's halfway?"

"You follow the rules and I won't get angry."

"Very funny." She tugged her hand free, but more
because she was shivering in a different way. Why did she
have to find him so appealing? He was all wrong for her.
He was imprisoning her, just like her father and brother
had, preventing her from living a normal life.

But he wasn't her father or brother. He was Zach, whose
touch excited her. Because it was forbidden? What was the
truth? She couldn't even trust her own emotions, her own
reactions to him.

She followed him back to the castle. At the bottom of

her staircase he stopped her from going farther by laying his hand on her arm.

"It won't be so bad," he said.

"Are you trying to convince me or yourself?"

For several long seconds he said nothing. Then slowly, carefully he moved closer. She stood her ground, not allowing him to intimidate her. Then he took her face in his hands and kissed her.

Stunned, she went perfectly still, but her lips parted as he prolonged the contact.

Was this what it would be like, being married to him? A constant temptation, without trust, without a future? Moments of thoughtfulness, like the gift of sheet music, followed by a kiss to distract her? Because that was surely what he was doing now.

And she couldn't resist him.

He stepped away just as she went up on tiptoe to bring herself closer.

"See? Not so bad," he said, then he turned and walked away.

"You said it would be in name only," she managed to say, the words almost sticking in her throat.

"You trusted a criminal?"

He was out of sight before her brain came up with a response. She plunked herself down on the staircase, dragged her fingers along her lips. It was just a form of brainwashing, a way to get her to accept an idea contrary to her own.

She couldn't let that happen. She had things to do, a life to live.

Julianne hurried upstairs and grabbed her cell phone.

"I need to leave," she said to Jamey when he answered.

"Hello to you, too, Julianne. Why do you need to leave this time?"

She thought she heard him sigh. She didn't want to be placated. She also couldn't tell him the truth. She'd broken Zach's trust once already. She wouldn't be responsible for breaking it again by telling Jamey her fears.

"I just want to go somewhere else. My reasons are important, but they're my own."

"All right. Give me a few days."

"No. Now. Tomorrow or the day after. No later."

"What the big rush?"

"Because it's…it's boring."

"You said that before. Then you changed your mind."

"This time it's different."

"I said okay. Be patient. It could take as much as a week."

A week? Panic set in. She had less than three days to find a way out of the marriage. "Not in a week. *Now*."

"Okay. Okay. Calm down. I'll give Zach a call. If you want to leave that fast, I'm going to need help on his end."

"Don't you dare call Zach."

A long silence ensued. "Why not?" he asked finally.

"Because I don't want him trying to change my mind. Just do it, okay?"

"What's going on, Julianne?"

"I just want off."

Another silence crackled between them. "I'll see what I can do."

After saying goodbye she hung up the phone. When she realized how rigid with stress she was, she forced herself to sit on the window seat and relax her body. When she finally let go of the tension she found herself filled with fear. Not fear of Zach. No, it was fear of losing herself. Of giving in when she'd just learned to take charge of her life in some small way.

She couldn't lose that.

"I have to fight you," she said aloud. "I have to."

She curled up on the window seat, clutching a pillow. Time for a new plan.

Zach glanced at the Caller ID when his phone rang. He stretched out on his bed, figuring he was in for a long conversation.

"What did you do to Julianne?" Jamey asked, not even saying hello.

"Told her she had to marry me."

A keening silence followed. *"You what?"*

"You heard me."

"I think you'd better tell me what happened."

Zach did, leaving out the fact he'd come to like her. How he'd come to listen for her footsteps and enjoy her playing the piano in the evening. How the living room seemed hollow and empty when he passed through it and she wasn't there. How he liked the way she took a step back from the dogs before she petted them, as if overcoming a fear first.

But liking her and trusting her were two different things. He'd already checked the history on her computer and found she was trying to find the name of an artist from the Prom. She was far too curious. How could he trust her with the details of what he did? She'd broken the only request he'd asked of her.

"If she only saw the pictures…" Jamey let the sentence drift.

"She recognized one of them. That changes everything.

I'm protecting *her*," Zach said, frustrated that Jamie wasn't getting it. "The last thing she needs in her life right now is to be interrogated and dragged into more criminal proceedings. She went through that because of her brother."

"And then the D.A. let her go. They figured they had enough evidence that her testimony wasn't necessary."

"Only because you called in favors. You convinced the D.A. not to put her on the stand."

"Sort of. It was a fine line. Her testimony might have helped. And she may yet be called. But I suppose it was a favor."

"I'm doing her a favor, too." Why couldn't Jamey see that? Why did Julianne refuse to see it, too? And didn't she realize he'd been holding back during the kiss? That he'd purposely not put his arms around her because he figured he wouldn't let go? The few times he'd touched her when he'd helped her climb to the bluff, he'd gotten a pretty good idea of how her body would feel up next to his, all curves and temptation.

Her blond hair may give her an angelic look, but her I'll-fight-you-all-the-way attitude countered it. The castle's atmosphere felt…buoyant now, reminding him that there had been happier times in his life. He couldn't afford those memories. He had to stay focused on the task at hand. The enormous, never-ending task at hand.

"Okay," Jamey said quietly.

"Okay? You're okay with it? You think I'm doing the right thing?"

"I think you're doing what you need to do."

Zach decided not to examine Jamey's words. "You won't help her get off the Prom?"

"I won't help."

"She's going to be furious."

"I'm not in throwing range."

Zach smiled finally and let himself relax. "What will you tell her?"

"That I can't help her."

"She's gonna love that."

"Fortunately, you have to deal with her, not me. Zach? I need a serious answer to something."

"Shoot."

"Do you have feelings for her?"

Feelings? Yeah. Graphic ones. Get-her-naked-and-in-bed feelings. But beyond that? He couldn't go there, had to stop thinking about how his life had already changed because of her—for better or for worse, he wasn't sure yet.

"I like her. I feel responsible for her because you asked me to, but I would feel responsible regardless. She's vulnerable and maybe susceptible. That's a dangerous combination."

"She would understand what you're doing."

"She doesn't need to know more than she already knows."

"Okay, okay. Just try not to hurt her."

"I try not to hurt anyone."

Zach set down the phone a few seconds later. He tucked his hands behind his head and stared at the ceiling. Truth time, he thought. Maybe marriage was a drastic solution, but he was a risk taker, a rule breaker. He had to be. The possibility of her having to testify against him wasn't a risk he would take.

No one in his care would ever suffer again. No one. He'd made it his life's goal.

And he never broke a promise.

Seven

Even under the circumstances, Julianne was thrilled to travel to Friday Harbor, a one-square-mile, population-2,000 city on the island called San Juan, which offered what she missed most—shopping, restaurants and people. And knowing Jamey was going to help her get off the island meant she could just relax and go along with Zach's demands.

They took care of the marriage license first. She didn't put up a fight, which earned her both his thanks and a frown, which she hoped didn't indicate that he knew what she was up to. Only the tiniest amount of guilt ran through her mind at her pretense. It wasn't as if people who got marriage licenses had a legal obligation to use them, after all.

"Would you like to buy something new to wear for the wedding?" he asked as they walked through the tourist section.

"I don't see why."

"You already have something appropriate?"

What would he consider appropriate? A long gown with a train? A veil? How could she do that? That was part of her dream. She needed to hold onto that dream for when the right man—

Why did Zach seem like the right man? Why did a hot little ache settle in her heart every time she thought about marrying him. She wasn't going to marry him. Period.

"I don't need anything new," she said for the sake of argument, not wanting to make anything too easy on him.

"It needs to look real. We'll have pictures taken. They'll be displayed. You should look like a bride."

"Maybe I'll wear my bikini."

His hesitation lasted two beats. "Suit yourself."

It wasn't much fun trying to get a rise out of him when he was...unrisable. He probably knew she wasn't about to miss out on the opportunity to shop. Was it a good thing that he knew her that well?

She let herself enjoy the temporary freedom. It felt wonderful being out, as if awakening from hibernation. She drank in the sights—people walking, saying hi to friends and acquaintances, laughing. Especially laughing.

She felt twenty pounds lighter as she and Zach ambled along. Then the front-window display of a shop caught her eye. Trendy clothes but not outrageous. She would buy something, after all. To keep him off track, to make him think she'd resigned herself to the wedding. She headed to the front door, then sensed him directly behind her.

"What do you think you're doing?" she asked, facing him.

"Coming with you."

"I don't need help shopping. In fact, the groom isn't supposed to see the bride before the wedding."

"As you keep pointing out, this isn't a real wedding," he said. "And if you think I'm giving you any opportunity to get away, when you've specifically told me you would try, you're crazy."

She did have a back-up plan, having decided she shouldn't completely depend on Jamey to do something she should be doing herself. Nothing was finalized yet, but she knew she couldn't get away from him on this island. She needed to get to the mainland. Anacordes.

"I can see from here that there's a back door to the shop," he added.

"Really, Zach, where would I go?"

"You're resourceful."

The compliment pleased her. "I promise I won't run."

He eyed her for several long seconds, as if challenging her promise as something he could believe in, then he held out his hand. "Your wallet."

She sighed dramatically and passed him her purse.

He recoiled. "Just your wallet."

She grinned. "Does it undermine your masculinity to hold my purse?"

He kept his hand out until she set her wallet there.

"Anyone tell you you're too serious?" she queried, then was sorry when his eyes dulled, as if she'd insulted him.

"Yes."

"Ever think about changing?"

"Never."

The word came without hesitation. So, why did she think he wasn't telling the truth? That he had, indeed, wanted to change. Something new lurked in his eyes, different from what she'd seen before. Not criticism or curiosity. Not exasperation or enjoyment. Not desire, either. Hope? A wish for himself?

Tenderness swamped her, unbidden and unwanted. "You have the power to do anything, Zach. To be different. To fulfill your dreams. What do you dream about?"

"I never dream."

Worse than she expected.

"I'll wait here for you," he said, his voice cool.

"I won't be long."

"Take your time."

She rejoined him an hour later, a dress bag in hand. They found a little market, bought some cheese and bread and apples, plus a bottle of Merlot and two glasses, then they sought out a park bench where they could watch the harbor as they shared the food.

They ate and talked and were quiet, too. Some gulls flew overhead, noisy and daring. Against Zach's caution, Julianne tossed chunks of bread to them. The birds got braver. One swooped over the picnic table and pulled the heel of the loaf over the edge, too heavy to carry off. Several birds attacked the hunk then squawked at her when there was nothing left.

Zach raised his brows at her, saying he'd told her so without saying the words. She laughed.

They cleaned up their trash. She realized that she hadn't had to pretend to have a good time with him. Because it seemed like the most natural thing in the world to do, she raised up on tiptoe and lightly touched her lips to his. He wrapped an arm around her, pulling her close, deepening the kiss.

"Get a room!" someone shouted from a passing car.

They broke the kiss but didn't move apart.

"We should get back to the Prom," he said, his arm dropping away from her waist.

She nodded, thoughtful, wondering, not for the first time, if she was making a mistake running out on him. Maybe they could make something of the relationship beyond his need that a wife not testify against her husband. He just needed the right woman—

What was she thinking? She wanted to finish college, actually attend classes on campus. She wanted to be independent and carefree. And eventually she wanted to marry a man who loved her, adored her, cherished her. A man who kept no secrets.

That man was worth waiting for.

At home later, Zach lurked near the dining room, awaiting Julianne's arrival for dinner. Their day in Friday Harbor had been long but surprisingly entertaining. She'd been in a good mood most of the time, had teased him, flirted with him, even kissed him once. He'd enjoyed her good spirits and the fact she didn't argue with him.

That was about to change.

An hour ago Jamey had called just as they arrived back at the castle. She'd said a cheerful hello into her cell phone then the color leeched from her face. It was apparent that Jamey was telling her he wasn't going to help her leave the island. Without a glance in Zach's direction she'd hurried up the tower stairs. She hadn't come out since.

"Should I tell her that dinner is ready?" Mrs. Moody asked, concern in her eyes.

"Yes, please."

A few minutes later, Mrs. Moody returned. "She says she's not hungry."

He forced a smile. "That's a first."

"Yes, sir."

"Thank you, Mrs. Moody."

She nodded then left. Now what? Should he give Julianne time to accept the forthcoming marriage—something he didn't believe she'd done, because she'd thought Jamey would help her leave the island. He'd gotten a taste today of life with her when she was happy, and he'd felt hope for the future, that at least they could live together peacefully until—

Until.

Now she would feel stuck. And everything would revert back to her initial reaction. She didn't want to marry him, to be saddled with him, even though it was for her own protection.

Surely she could see that it was more of a benefit to her so that she didn't have to go to court again, and admit to being associated with a criminal again. And this case would garner a whole lot more media attention than her brother's had.

She didn't see it that way, of course. He couldn't really explain it to her, either. The less she knew, the more protected she was.

Or was that just an excuse?

He didn't want to examine that idea, so he climbed the stairs to her room instead and knocked.

She opened the door. He'd expected her to be angry. Instead, she looked…worn out. Or maybe resigned.

"What?" she asked, crossing her arms.

"Mrs. Moody said you weren't hungry. I was checking to see if you're okay."

"I'm tired."

"It was a long day."

"I'm going to bed early."

At seven o'clock? "Would you like to go for a walk?"

"No, thank you."

He reached into his back pocket and pulled out the granola bar he'd grabbed on his way through the kitchen. "Just in case," he said, passing it to her.

Her eyes welled. What the hell? It was just a granola bar.

"I can't let you win, Zach," she whispered.

Ah. She wasn't done fighting him, after all. What next? And would he admire her as much if she didn't fight?

"This wasn't part of your plan."

She brushed at the tears that spilled down her cheeks. "Or my dreams."

He decided he didn't want her to explain that. "I'll see you at breakfast?"

"Sure."

"Good night."

The door closed slowly behind him as he went down the stairs, as if she didn't have enough strength to just shut it. He stopped in the kitchen. "I'll have dinner now, Mrs. Moody."

"Yes, sir."

"And if you would, please take Julianne a mocha in a little while."

"I'd be happy to. She's doing better, then?"

"She'll be fine."

He had to keep a closer eye on her now. She had two days left to get out of the marriage. He was sure she would make the most of that time.

Julianne figured only one option remained for her. She had to find a way to leave the island by boat. She knew no resident would give her a ride, so her only hope was the man who brought the mail. However, since he pulled right up to the dock where Lil could see him from her store, Julianne's chances of talking to him alone were slim.

But if she didn't try, she wouldn't forgive herself.

"I'm going to Lil's," she announced to Mrs. Moody after lunch. Mr. Moody and Zach had left on foot a while ago, heading toward where the helicopter always landed. "Do you need anything?"

"Nothing, thanks. Are you taking the Jeep?"

"That's okay, isn't it?"

"I don't see why not."

Mrs. Moody opened a cupboard door and chose a key ring with a single key on it. On the next hook was the boat key attached to a floating bobber. Could she? Did she dare?

No. Even if she stole the key and somehow started the motor, she didn't know where to head, especially at night, which was her only hope—late at night, while everyone slept. She wasn't foolish enough to think she could do that.

A while later she wandered into Lil's, passed the time eating brownies and drinking coffee. Finally the mail boat came.

"Oh, I forgot a letter I brought with me," Julianne said. "I'll get it from the Jeep."

She retrieved the letter and walked slowly to the dock, giving Lil and the man time to talk, hoping he would just take her letter and go. Lil lingered, laughing. Flirting? Julianne turned the envelope upside down and passed it to him.

Please don't turn it over yet. But please look at it later. Please.

He tucked it in his bag then waved goodbye. Julianne took her first deep breath in minutes. She managed to smile at Lil but left right away. Julianne was taking a big risk, but it was her only shot.

Sometime tonight she would have her answer—if he sorted the mail himself and found her note. And if he was willing.

She checked her cell phone to make sure it was on.

Then she waited.

The call came just before dinner.

"Meet me at midnight at the dock," he said in a raspy whisper, as if someone might overhear.

"I'll be there." She had already packed a bag, just one, traveling light.

Regret tried to push through the wall of relief she felt. She would leave the island at midnight. She would disappear for as long as she could stand it. She wouldn't even let Jamey know where she was.

After a while Zach would forget all about her.

But she would never forget him.

Julianne saw the boat's running lights just before midnight. She was crouched low but stood as the boat neared. She walked down the wood planks to the end of the dock, the darkness terrifying.

The boat's motor decelerated. Her pulse pounded. Nausea made her light-headed. He tossed a line to her. She grabbed it and pulled him close. A canvas top protected him from a drizzle that had started an hour ago. She tossed her canvas bag into the back of the boat. The man stood, extended his hand.

"Going somewhere, Julianne?"

She stumbled back. Zach! How did he— Who told— Her shoulders slumped. She should've known. Everyone was loyal to him. Everyone.

She plopped onto the dock. He hopped out of the boat and sat beside her.

"That's it," she said, for some reason not angry or even disappointed. She'd given it her best shot. It just wasn't good enough. She didn't have his resources.

"Nice try," he said lightly.

She smiled and shrugged. "Thanks."

"As I said before, you're resourceful. And daring."

"And foolish, I suppose."

He shook his head. "I admire you."

"Do you?"

"Yeah." He brushed her damp hair back from her face. "You've certainly made my life interesting."

"I have, haven't I?"

He nodded. "Ready to go home?"

"Ready."

"No more attempts to escape?"

"I have one more day, Zach."

He laughed, an exasperated sound. She realized she loved the sound, and that she was responsible for it.

"Did he call you?" she asked after they stood.

"On his way back to Anacordes."

Something in his tone of voice alerted her. "You guessed I would approach him, didn't you?"

"You didn't have many options."

She sighed. He didn't have to worry. She was done attempting a getaway. Her fate was sealed. It helped that Jamey had insisted Zach was a good man. Did Jamey really know what Zach did?

It didn't matter. None of it did. Because she was about to become Mrs. Zachary Keller. Nothing could stop it now.

Eight

Forced to the altar. Julianne paced in her room. It seemed so…archaic when she thought of it that way. Ridiculous. Impossible. What would happen if she said, "I don't?"

Mr. Moody would come get her for the ceremony any minute now. Her nerves were stretched thin, even though she'd resigned herself to the marriage, had accepted her fate, had come to an understanding with Zach that the marriage would happen.

But there was also an uncontrolled something or other inside her that seemed to be rebelliously excited and curious about marrying Zach. She told herself it was reaction to his kiss, to the magnetic pull she'd felt for him from the beginning, and the sheer mystery of who he was.

But that wasn't all.

She wanted to know what he did that made him a criminal. And how Jamey, a private investigator, would be friends with someone who knowingly and consistently broke the law. It was a puzzle she wanted, needed, to solve.

Julianne heard footsteps coming up her stairs. She froze momentarily, then looked in the mirror. Her hair had co-operated, the curls relaxed and shiny. Her nails were painted Flamingo Pink, although she wore a softer shade on her lips. Unfamiliar emotions were reflected in her face, her skin pale and her eyes huge with the unknown. Her pulse thundered.

The footsteps gained in volume. Mr. Moody reached the top step, the landing, then came his knock. Her stomach lurched. This was not at all how she'd pictured herself getting married. She'd wanted time on her own first. Lots of it, with no one to answer to. She'd gotten none in her entire life, except a small taste when she lived in San Francisco, away from her brother but still under his control.

"Miss?" Mr. Moody called out after another quick knock.

"I'll be right there."

She pressed a hand to her stomach and blew out a breath. Whoever said such things would calm you was out of their mind. She felt as scared and worried and flustered as before.

But she could rise above it.

Shoulders back she pulled open the door. Mr. Moody stood there looking formal and solemn in a black suit, white shirt and black tie. He shoved a bouquet at her.

"From Mr. Zach," he said.

Every cell in her body sighed. She buried her face in the mostly roses bouquet. The fragrance drifted through her, imprinting itself in her mental scrapbook of memories.

Mr. Moody crooked an arm in invitation. Awkwardly she

took it. Neither of them spoke. Her three-inch heels seemed like stilts. She was grateful she could hang on to him during the descent of the staircase as her knees wobbled.

I can do this. I can do this. The words repeated and recycled, giving her strength.

They reached the bottom. He patted her hand and smiled at her—a small one, but a smile nonetheless. "My wife and I wish you all the happiness in the world."

"Thank you," she said, surprised and wary. Hadn't Zach told them it was a marriage in name only?

They walked through the kitchen and dining room then approached the living room. She spotted Zach standing next to a man with graying hair, the judge who would perform the ceremony, Julianne decided. A few people were scattered around the room—Misery sat at the piano, Reb on the sofa, along with two people she didn't know. Several more seats were taken up by strangers.

Mrs. Moody approached Julianne. "I'll be moving your things into the master suite right after the ceremony. You don't worry about a thing."

Julianne's throat closed. She would be sleeping with Zach? No way. Absolutely no way. She couldn't have that temptation—or the pain of him rejecting her. Which was worse? She didn't know. Didn't want to find out.

Lil came from out of nowhere. She wore a sapphire-blue dress and carried a small rose bouquet similar to Julianne's. Julianne couldn't utter a sound.

"I'm honored you invited me to be your maid of honor," Lil said quietly. "Surprised, but honored. You know, you could've asked me yourself instead of having Zach do it. Maybe I haven't known you long but I think you know I like you." She glanced around the room. "You don't have any family attending? One day's notice probably wasn't enough, I guess."

Family. Julianne stared at Zach standing fifteen feet away, his face expressionless. What have you done? she wanted to scream.

She looked at everyone else, one by one. Smiles, expectation and curiosity shimmered from all of them, whether or not the face was familiar.

Then with panic shoving her with insistent hands, she turned and ran toward the side door, intent on finding fresh air to breathe before she passed out.

Zach didn't get caught off guard often, but seeing Julianne run rooted him in place. He'd been admiring her, from her golden curls to her simple white, knee-length dress, to her spiky high heels. He'd seen her look around the room, noting the others in attendance. She'd visibly shrunk back from the scene, then when Lil approached her, Julianne took actual steps back, her eyes widening. Then she'd hightailed it out of the room.

Zach didn't run but he didn't walk, either.

"Maybe I should talk to her," Lil said as he passed by. "Jitters, probably."

"I'll do it," he said, trying not to sound too brusque or dismissing. He didn't know what Julianne would say to Lil, how much she would reveal.

"The groom's not supposed to—"

Zach ignored Lil. When he was out of the guests' sight he picked up speed, taking the steps to the tower room two at a time. The room was empty. He looked out the window and spotted her hurrying toward the trail to the bluff, but making slow progress in her heels.

He caught up with her before she'd gone far at all.

"Go away," she said without turning. "Leave me alone."

"I can't." He came up beside her, keeping pace. "What's wrong?"

"You have to ask that?"

"If I want to know the answer."

She skidded to a stop and plunked her fists on her hips, her bouquet still tucked in one hand, the ribbons trailing down her dress. "You could've warned me."

Damn he wanted to kiss her, to feel that fierce passion against his mouth. "About what?"

"About the people you invited to what I thought was a marriage of appearances and alibis. About Lil being my maid of honor! It wasn't supposed to be a wedding, Zach."

"What was it supposed to be?"

"A ceremony. Legal and binding to the world, but still fake."

"And so it is."

Her mouth drew into a hard line. "I don't get it."

"We can't risk being accused of marrying for 'appearances and alibis,' as you called it. It has to seem like a real marriage, a loving relationship. We needed witnesses to our *happiness*."

"You idiot," she growled, low and frustrated.

"I beg your pardon?"

"You heard me. Why didn't you just say so? Why blindside me with it?"

"Because I figured you would balk."

"And knocking the wind out of me was preferable? Don't you know anything about women?"

Obviously not. And less about her, as well.

"And what's this about me moving into your suite?" she

went on, getting in his face. "You didn't think you should talk that over with me, either?"

"I didn't…think."

That, at least, stopped her from yelling.

"I figured you had a computer for a brain," she muttered, backing down.

"Far from it."

"Tell me what you do, Zach. Help me understand who you are."

"I'm doing a good thing. I can't tell you more. I'm helping. But now we need to get back to the wedding."

She stared at him for several long, searching seconds. When she finally spoke it was from behind a barrier of his own making, a wall of iron, invisible but just as hard to break through as the real thing.

"Yes, sir," she said, ice coating the words.

By sheer force of will he didn't sigh. "I hope you'll put on a happy face for our guests."

"*Your* guests."

"You're being childish, Julianne." He regretted the words instantly as hurt flickered in her eyes. Yes, she'd defied him, which had led to this fake marriage in the first place, but he hadn't been considerate, either. And he should be. "I'm sor—"

"You've treated me like a child," she said, cool and distant. "But I'll walk in there with you and stand beside you and pledge my *love* in the biggest lie of my life. Then you can ignore me, and I'll ignore you until such time as it's possible to annul the marriage and I can leave."

He didn't want that. He didn't want them to ignore each other, to be strangers. He liked her. When she chose to, she could make him laugh. He didn't want her to feel like a prisoner, even if she was one. "Thank you," he said.

"No problem."

Flippant words and a condescending tone. He obviously had work ahead of him to make amends.

They returned to the castle, put on the requisite happy faces and made promises they wouldn't keep, making a mockery of the vows in the process. Zach had broken so many laws, he'd lost count, but reciting those vows seemed more criminal than anything he'd done. Sealing it with a wedding ring did nothing to ease his guilt.

"I now pronounce you husband and wife," the judge intoned. "You may kiss your bride."

They faced each other. She no longer looked belligerent. Instead, she raised her brows as if daring him.

"Come on, kiss her!" Misery shouted.

Her smile became a challenge. He'd wipe that smile off her face—and give the locals a story to spread. No bride would be kissed as thoroughly. That he was indulging his own desires was merely coincidental.

He cupped her head with his hands and moved in. His lips brushed hers, lingered, then settled. He slipped his arms around her, felt hers wrap around him hesitantly, then like a vise. Catcalls filled the room as the kiss heated and deepened, then he heard nothing at all, except a soft sigh when he lifted his head to change the angle of the kiss.

One sigh, hushed but full of need. It was enough to stop him, to remind him of the precariousness of their relationship and the people watching them. He did not want to embarrass Julianne—or lose the respect of the residents of the Prom, each of whom held a special place in his life.

Holding her shoulders, he stepped back. She recovered

quickly and well, pretending to be the blushing bride, when she was probably furious.

Well-wishers gathered around them. Mrs. Moody had prepared a feast. Laughter and conversation filled the room, a rare sound, Zach realized, and a good one. He watched his…"wife" as she joked with Lil and Misery while nibbling from a plate piled with delicacies—shrimp, caviar, ahi and slivers of tender beef. She popped a stuffed olive in her mouth. Her mouth too full to talk, she listened, her eyes smiling, as Lil told a story.

After a while Julianne's gaze landed on Zach and seemed to beg him, but for what? He went to her, slid his arm around her waist, pressed his lips to her hair, as fragrant as a spring garden. She leaned against him.

"Tired?" he whispered.

She nodded. It was only five o'clock, too soon to retire, and the guests didn't seem in any hurry to leave. He glanced at Lil.

She winked. "Okay, everybody," she said over the crowd noise. "I think we should take this show on the road. The newlyweds would like some time together, so grab whatever open bottles are left and let's head to my place."

"Let me package up some food," Mrs. Moody said.

A flurry of activity ensued—food packed, goodbyes said, some final jabs at Zach's loss of bachelorhood issued. Finally, quiet.

"Your things have been moved," Mrs. Moody told Julianne, then turned to Zach. "Dinner is in the refrigerator, along with heating instructions. We'll see you tomorrow around noon."

Zach felt Julianne stiffen beside him but she said nothing.

"Thank you. Thank you for everything you did to make

this happen today," Zach said to the Moodys. He didn't know what he would do without them, without their forgiveness and their unconditional love.

Mr. Moody shook his hand, then Julianne's. Mrs. Moody kissed Zach's cheek, then hugged Julianne, who couldn't hide her surprise at the gesture.

The house rang with silence.

"Where are they going?" Julianne asked.

"To Lil's, overnight. To give us privacy."

She stepped out of her high heels, wiggled her toes and groaned. "Then I'll sleep in my own room. Good night."

What the hell? He caught up with her after only a few steps, swooped her into his arms and carried her to the sofa. She didn't fight him physically, but she gave him an earful. He plunked her down, then held her there when she tried to spring up.

"It's time we get a few things straight," he said. "Mrs. Keller."

Nine

So, the kid gloves were coming off, Julianne thought. Good. Some honesty between them might help settle things.

She crossed her arms. "Go ahead. Set me straight, *Mr.* Keller."

"First of all, to the rest of the world, this marriage is real. Only you and I know the reason for it."

"And everyone else thinks we fell in love in a week and simply *had* to get married? I think these people know you too well to believe that."

"They'll believe whatever I tell them."

"Don't expect the same of me."

"If you let on to anyone that this marriage is other than real, you put that person in jeopardy. Do you want that on your shoulders?"

Of course she didn't. "No."

"Okay. Second, in order for this to appear like the real thing, we have to share a room."

"I understand. But we don't have to share a bed."

"Mrs. Moody makes the bed. She cleans the room. She's in there every day. Where would I put a cot or whatever?"

"Sleeping bags roll up and can be hidden in a closet."

"I'm not sleeping on the floor. You can, if you like."

He didn't see that she wasn't worried about *him* taking advantage. She was worried about herself. Unless he continued on as a dictator, like now.

When she didn't answer, he added, "It's a big bed. We don't have to touch."

He must have a lot of faith that she wouldn't act on her attraction, even unknowingly in her sleep. The nights were cold, and getting longer…

"Agreed?" he asked.

"Sure." Like she had a choice?

"Outside the room, we need to look like newlyweds."

"Whatever." If she acted bored, would he believe she wasn't getting aroused just thinking about sleeping in the same bed, touching him in the hallways as they passed, sharing meals and conversations? "Is there more?"

"I need to know that what happens in this house, stays in this house. I will protect you from as much as I can, but the longer you're here, the more you'll see. You can't talk about it with anyone. Not Jamey. Not Lil. Not even the Moodys."

"I won't disappoint you again."

Tension left him like a balloon losing air, slowly, steadily, visibly. "Thank you."

"I'm going to change out of these clothes." She headed to the staircase. She knew which room was his, but she hadn't seen inside it, as the door was always closed. And then there was the door that led to the other tower room, where someone lived. No ghost, but a woman.

Julianne needed to remember that Zach had secrets she might never learn about. Deep, dark secrets, with consequences.

She sighed as she climbed the stairs. Her feet ached.

"You looked beautiful, Julianne," he said from where he stood.

The sincerity of the compliment brought heat to her body. For moments of time today she'd felt like a bride, and she'd liked having his arm around her, and his lips on hers. But because she'd lived her life playing a role, first for her father then for her brother, she resented that she had to play a role at all.

Still, she wanted to keep the peace with him, so she thanked him and continued up the stairs.

She turned the doorknob to his room. Everything was… big—a huge, eighteenth-century stone fireplace, colorful tapestries and the bed. He was right. It was large enough that they wouldn't touch…unless they wanted to.

"Your clothes will be in the closet behind the door on the right," he said from close behind her, startling her. "And in the left armoire."

"Thanks."

"What would you like to do for the evening?"

Have a wedding night. The thought triggered electrical charges in her erogenous zones. She didn't understand it. She hardly knew him. Sometimes she didn't even like him—or maybe she just resented another man being in charge over her, controlling her.

Yet she wanted him.

"Maybe just go for a walk," she said finally, moving toward the closet, needing to get out of range of his body heat.

"It's raining."

"Really?" She looked toward a window. "When did that start?"

"During the reception."

She heard laughter in his voice and smiled a little in return. "I hadn't noticed."

He kindly didn't tease her but instead grabbed jeans and a sweater from a dresser. "I'll leave you to change." He closed the door.

His walk-in closet was enormous, and her clothes hung neatly inside, with room to dress there, as well. After she changed she found him leaning against the wall outside the bedroom. "You hungry?" he asked.

"I could eat."

He wouldn't let her help heat up the dinner that Mrs. Moody left behind, an amazing lobster thermador, crisp green salad and homemade rolls. They carried the food to the dining room but conversation lagged. She didn't know what she could ask him, so she asked nothing.

Just as they settled in the media room to watch an old Katherine Hepburn/Spencer Tracy movie, the phone rang. He listened for a moment, then pressed the hold button.

"I have to take this in the office," he said. "Go ahead and start the movie without me." He didn't wait for a response.

Feeling abandoned, she curled up on the couch to watch the movie. She toyed with her wedding ring, a stunning circle of diamonds. She hadn't expected such a ring, if she'd considered it, she would've. But she would've assumed he'd buy a plain gold band. Instead it looked like a real token of love and commitment—the "appearances" part of the marriage. It made her sad.

An hour later Zach returned.

"I need you to stay in this room for a while," he said abruptly.

"How long?"

"Maybe an hour. If you'd rather be in the bedroom, go now, but please stay put."

"Bedroom," she said, standing. She could see outside from there.

"Go quickly."

She jogged up the stairs and slammed the door shut. After a minute she heard the helicopter. Breathless she ran to the window and watched its spotlight light up the landing area. The rain had stopped. She saw Zach make his way quickly up the path then disappear. As she had before, she waited and waited for his return.

Julianne went still as she heard a baby cry, the sound thready through the stone walls but definitely a baby, or toddler, crying.

What was going on? Obviously the helicopter had brought a child, but why? What secret, criminal thing did Zach do involving children? He couldn't possibly be harming them—or anyone—so…what? What?

She pressed her ear to the door. It opened suddenly, making her stumble back, and the sound of crying filled the room.

"Know anything about babies?" Zach asked over the noise. He tucked the screaming child closer to him.

She automatically patted the child's back. "Not really."

"You probably know more than I do. Here. His name is Jacob." He plunked the boy into a perplexed Julianne's arms. "I'll be right back."

Jacob pushed and shoved and kicked and wriggled. He screamed and cried. Tears ran down his face. Julianne walked and jostled and hushed, again and again and again. He was the first baby she'd held. She hadn't babysat or had nieces or nephews or cousins to care for. Was she holding him too tight? Too loose? Too…wrong? Why was he here without his mother?

Where is Zach?

He flew in carrying diapers and other paraphernalia.

"I hope you brought one of those pacifier things," she shouted.

"Maybe." He dug into a bag and came up with one.

She snatched it out of his hand and slipped it into Jacob's open mouth midscream. It fell out. She tried again, rubbing it against the inside of his cheeks. His lips clamped shut around it and he sucked hard and noisily. Poor thing. His big blue eyes finally focused on her. Tears trailed into his soft, shiny brown hair, soaking it. She smiled at him. He sniffled, his breath hitching, then his eyes began to close. Poor thing had worn himself out. She kissed his forehead…and recognized him.

"Thank you," Zach said quietly.

She'd forgotten he was there. So many questions came to mind. Would he answer them? "His picture is on the wall in your office."

There was a long pause, then, "Yes."

Yes. A simple and complicated word. "How old is he?"

"Fifteen months."

"Why do you have him?"

"Someone else would've taken care of him, but they weren't available."

"That's not an answer, Zach." Jacob became dead

weight in her arms, but she didn't want to put him down, thinking he needed the comfort she offered, and feeling, well, possessive. She'd stopped his crying, after all. It was her face he'd seen before he fell asleep. She figured he should wake up to the same face.

She tucked Jacob closer then spoke to Zach. "I think it's time you tell me what's going on."

He ran his hands through his hair. She waited. Finally he spoke. "Four weeks ago Jacob's father kidnapped him. We just recovered him."

"We?"

"My team."

"Are you some kind of law enforcement?"

"The opposite."

"I don't understand."

"We have no legal authorization to do what we do."

"Which is?"

"We rescue the abducted."

So, he *was* a good guy. Relief blanketed her. "As a full-time job?"

"Unfortunately, yes, it has become that."

"The pictures on the wall in your office…?"

"Are current cases. And successes. And failures."

She wondered whether the wall with the huge number of photos was the success or failure wall.

A phone rang. He pulled his portable out of his pocket and answered it. "Okay, good… He's sleeping. Thanks." He ended the call. "Julianne, I promise I'll explain more to you, but right now Jacob's mother is arriving and things are going to get hectic for a little while."

"What can I do to help?"

He laid a hand on her shoulder. Gratitude shone in his

eyes. "We're a well-oiled machine. What would help most is if you would stay out of the way. I know that sounds harsh—"

She put a hand over his mouth. "No. It's okay. Just tell me if you need me for anything. I think— I think what you do is noble."

He kissed her, lightly at first, then he pulled her as close as he could get her with Jacob in her arms and deepened the kiss, until she was giddy and light headed…and needy.

"We'll talk later," he said, stepping back then hurrying away.

She looked down at the sweet little boy. She wondered how Zach knew that Jacob was better off with his mother than his father. She assumed he checked out that sort of thing. She hadn't figured him for a particularly emotional man, but a practical one. His passion for his work told her there was a deeper story, maybe a sad one.

That made him even more intriguing.

And now she was married to him…

Ten

It had been a long night. Zach stood outside his bedroom door, the castle quiet at last. Jacob and his mother were settled in the tower room that Julianne had just vacated. The Moodys were back, with looks of sympathy that his wedding night had been interrupted, but happy that Jacob had been found. That took precedence over everything, for everyone.

And now he would join his wife in bed for the first time, without the privileges of marriage, but with all the temptation.

He was proud of her, grateful to her. She'd stayed in the background, didn't ask questions, didn't approach him at all. She'd helped Mrs. Moody prepare food for the people involved and offered quiet smiles along with heaping plates and full mugs.

She'd gone to bed an hour ago, at 2:45 a.m., but before she had she'd tracked him down and given him a hug. He'd appreciated it. The usual fallout had already begun—Jacob's father was filing charges. They would face a too-familiar and exhausting battle.

He pushed open the door. Light spilled from the bathroom into the room. She'd left the light on and the door ajar. He glanced at the bed as he headed to the bathroom. She made a barely visible mound on the far side, under the down comforter. She was so close to the edge, he thought she might fall off if she moved another inch.

She would've been better off putting a rolled-up blanket or something down the middle of the bed. At least then she could spread out in the space it would create.

A few minutes later he climbed into bed. He lay on his side, facing her. The scent of her perfume just barely reached him, but his awareness of her was complete.

The sheets rustled as she rolled onto her back. "Are you okay?" she asked, her voice sleepy.

"I'm fine, thanks."

She yawned. "Will you be able to sleep?"

"If I say no, what would you do?" The question hung there like an invitation.

"Find you a sleeping pill."

He heard the smile in her voice. "I'm sure I'll fall asleep without resorting to that."

A surprisingly comfortable silence settled between them.

"Zach?" she whispered after a while.

"What?"

"I'm very proud to know you."

His throat swelled. People had said things like that to him before, but they were people whose friend or family member he and his team had rescued. He never saw his work as altruistic but a necessity.

He didn't have the words to answer Julianne's, so he slid a hand across the bed. She followed suit. Soon their fingers touched, then he wrapped his hand around hers and held tight.

They slept.

Zach was gone when Julianne woke up, lying not on her own side of the bed, not even in the middle, but halfway onto Zach's, her head on the edge of his pillow. She buried her face in it, but she couldn't conjure up any scent that seemed like him.

Had she rolled that close to him during the night? She didn't remember. Surely she would remember that.

She saw that it was ten-fifteen and wondered what was happening. Were Jacob and his mother still there? How about the helicopter pilot and crewman, who hadn't been introduced to her nor called by name?

She shoved the blankets aside and headed to the shower, which was double the size of the one in the tower room, giving her plenty of room. Anxious to get downstairs, she didn't take the time to dry her hair.

Julianne was greeted by quiet. No sounds from the kitchen. No baby crying. She went from room to room but found no one. She knocked on Zach's office door. Nothing.

She grabbed her jacket and went outside. Just then the Jeep came up the road, Zach at the wheel.

"Hey, sleepyhead," he said as he climbed out of the vehicle.

"Where is everyone?"

He sort of smiled. "I guess the honeymoon is over."

She tucked her hands in her pockets. "Sorry. You are somebody, but I meant everyone else. Jacob." She felt amazingly protective of the boy, since she'd been the one to stop him crying. She would remember his big, scared eyes forever.

"Jacob and his mother have been taken to a safe place. They'll stay there until the legal ramifications are dealt with. Mr. and Mrs. Moody returned to Lil's so that we could have time together." He approached Julianne, stopping a few inches from her. "Good morning."

"Hi." Did I move into your space while you were still in bed? she wanted to ask.

"Sleep well?"

"Very." Was that laughter lurking in his eyes? The blue hue seemed to shimmer.

She attempted to act blasé. "Something on your mind, Zach?"

"You're a bit of a bed hog, aren't you?"

So. She *had* crept to his side. The heat of embarrassment enveloped her. "I apologize."

"No, don't." He tugged on a still-damp curl, then cupped her face, his thumb brushing her cheek. "There's something between us. Might as well acknowledge it."

"What good would that do?"

"Keeps things honest. You admit there's an attraction?"

"Yes," she answered carefully, not giving him more.

He moved a little closer, so that they almost touched. "I'm going to bed…to sleep for a while."

It was an invitation without him putting either of them on the spot. "Sleep well," she said.

He smiled slowly, dragged his hands down her arms, then walked away. She didn't move until long after the door shut. What had his smile meant? That he could read her mind? That she might resist him today but not forever? Well, she knew that. The longer she stayed, the bigger the temptation.

But she had plans. They didn't include making love

with Zach Keller, even with the legal right—and the desire—to do so. It would only make it harder to leave, and leave she must. She couldn't live this isolated existence, no matter how important his job was. She needed people and activity and…life, the things she'd missed for so long.

Julianne finally went into the house. She walked through the kitchen and dining room then stood at the bottom of the staircase, her hand resting on the newel post. Was he right that they should acknowledge their attraction? Now that he'd admitted to being drawn to her, her own feelings had changed a little, finding freedom in his openness.

It was the mystery about him that had piqued her interest at first. Well, that and the fact he was gorgeous. The less he told her, the more she'd wanted to know. Now she knew what he did, although not what drove him to it. And he'd become more attractive, because he put other people first. She hadn't known many people like that in her life.

She believed he would even give up his own life for any of the strangers he'd helped rescue. Which made him a better person than she. Who would she die for? No one. There was no one. That would change someday, when she had children. But to die for a cause? No. In that regard, he was a much better person than she.

That revelation made it easier to stay away from him. That and remembering there was a woman locked in the tower room.

Julianne wandered into the media room and turned on the television, but the screen went unwatched as she stared into space and analyzed her situation.

Zach took care of a lot of people. He deserved to have someone take care of him. She could do that for a while—

for as long as she was there. It would be a repayment of sorts for providing her with a safe place to live. Not that she wouldn't enjoy herself in the process, of course…

She was rationalizing, justifying her own need to be with him. But all rationalization aside, it seemed like destiny, which is why her feelings had sprung to life after such a short time of knowing him. She'd been sent here because she needed something—shelter and protection— yet she'd found someone needier.

She sat up straight. Jamey had said something along those lines. He'd set them up to meet! Because Zach needed someone like her, Jamey had said.

That settled it. Julianne headed up the stairs. She inched open the door to the master bedroom, tiptoed in and shut the door quietly. He was sprawled on his back in the big bed, the comforter pulled to his shoulders. His bare shoulders. Last night he'd worn a T-shirt and sweatpants. Was he wearing anything at all now?

She inched closer to the bed. He sprung up, his hands fisted, body rigid. Then he saw it was her and relaxed.

"Change your mind?" he asked, his tone seeming almost sympathetic, as if he knew her decision was almost out of her control.

She nodded.

"Sleepy?"

She shook her head.

"Ah." He lifted the comforter and slid over, inviting her.

She toed off her shoes, then caught a glimpse of boxer shorts as she slipped under the covers. He wrapped her in the comforter and his arms and held her.

"I'm glad you came," he said softly.

She'd made the right decision. He needed someone to

care about him. She could do that, even though it would
hurt to leave him. But he made sacrifices, and so could she.

Oh, yeah, big sacrifice. Totally selfless. Right.

Well, she could think of it that way.

He found her lips with his, tenderly, arousingly. His
were so soft and warm. His tongue dipped into her mouth
and gently explored. She wound her arms around his neck
and dragged herself closer, her breathing choppy. She
moaned when he trailed his tongue down her neck,
coming back up to her ear, sucking the lobe into his
mouth, his heated breath chilling her damp skin. When he
returned to her mouth it was with more passion, more intensity, but he didn't seem in any hurry to move from step
to step.

He drew back. His gaze locked with hers, he set a hand
on her stomach then slid it over a breast. She sucked in air
and closed her eyes. He searched her with gentle hands.

"I pictured you," he said softly. "Before you came here.
I saw your clothes, touched them. I knew what your body
would be like."

She should've been annoyed at the intrusion into her
privacy, but she was too aroused to complain. "So you
weren't disappointed?"

"Why would I be?"

"I'm not—I don't have a model's body."

"You have a woman's body. Did someone criticize you?"

"It doesn't matter." She tried to draw him down to kiss
him but he resisted.

"You're beautiful. Perfect. Don't let anyone convince
you differently." He settled his hand on her breast. She
lifted toward him as he sought the contours of her nipple
through her sweater.

A moment later he peeled the sweater over her head. She was glad she'd worn her black lacy panties and bra, especially when he found her nipple through the lace and tugged on it with his teeth, gently but thoroughly, as he unzipped her jeans and shoved them down her legs. Her body shook; she could barely draw a full breath. He surrounded her with his touch and his scent, creating a world all their own. His breathing lost its steady rhythm. She moved her hands over his torso, feeling the definition of muscles, enjoying his smooth, warm skin. Her fingertips drifted to his waistband and lingered there, afraid to go lower. He grabbed her hand and moved it to blanket him, holding her palm against him as he moved.

She glanced at his face, at the tension that made it seem like he was in pain. She wanted to soothe him, to bring him peace.

He covered her body with his, moving her legs apart, fitting himself. Even with fabric between them she felt the length and breadth of him. He dragged out the moment, slowing down then picking up the pace again, then stopping before starting over again. Then he knelt, pulling her up with him. Reaching around to unclasp her bra he looked into her eyes.

"You're on the pill, right?" he asked, his voice hoarse.

A bit of the haze of arousal cleared. "No."

"Why not?"

"I haven't…had the need."

"You've been celibate?"

"Kind of."

"Kind of? How can you be kind of celibate?"

"Okay, totally."

"For how long?"

She set her hands on his chest and looked him in the eye. "Twenty-three years."

His hands dropped away from her bra clasp. "You're a virgin?"

"You say that like it's a curse."

"Julianne, you were going to let me make love to you."

Why was he speaking in the past tense? "Yes, so?"

"Why?"

Because you need me. "Because I want to. What does my lack of experience have to do with anything, Zach? It was bound to change sometime. Why not with you?"

"It's not 'lack of experience,' as you put it. It's the fact you'd be giving up your virginity to me. *Me.*"

"My husband."

"Your partner in 'appearances and alibis.'"

She could see she was losing this battle. "It's my choice."

"And it's mine not to accept the gift." He left the bed, grabbed his jeans from a chair and put them on, then T-shirt, sweater, shoes. Armored up, he returned to the bed and sat beside her. She'd tucked the comforter under her chin.

"Don't look at me like that," he said, brushing her hair from her face.

"Like what?"

"Like I ran over your dog."

She smiled against her will. "I...complicated things."

"You did. But it's okay."

She fluttered her eyelashes. "I did enjoy it."

"Brat."

"Think you can resist forever?" She felt a little braver, like she could be direct and not make him mad.

"It won't be forever, Julianne."

She hated that tolerant tone. "But you said you don't

know how long we'll stay married. What if it's years? You'd deny me my right to companionship during the prime years of my life?"

"I think your prime years come later. You won't miss out." He headed toward the door.

"Would you tell me about Hannah?" she said in a hurry, then held her breath as he stopped. She saw him tense. When he turned around, he'd lost all sense of the ease he'd had with her just moments ago.

"How do you know about Hannah?" His voice was low and harsh.

It had been a shot in the dark—and instinct. It was the only woman's name she found in her research that fit the *H___H* signature on the pen-and-ink drawings at Lil's. Not only was Julianne right, but she'd hit a nerve, a deep and sensitive one.

When she didn't answer, he moved toward her. "Hannah is not open for discussion. Not now. Not ever. You got that?"

She shrank back. "I got it." She shouldn't have brought it up yet. She should've enjoyed the new, warm relationship between them first, built some trust.

He stalked out of the room, pulling the door hard behind him.

One step forward, Julianne thought. And two steps back. The story of her life.

Zach shut himself in his office. Since there were no windows he couldn't focus on anything other than the photographs on the wall, but they faded into the background as he worked at getting control of his anger.

How did she know? How the hell did she know about Hannah? Had she overheard Mr. and Mrs. Moody talking?

He found that hard to believe. Had she been sneaking around? He couldn't imagine that— Well, maybe he could, but he still couldn't figure out what her sneaking would've accomplished, how she could've discovered information about Hannah.

He paced. Hannah had recently begun to be…difficult. Unpredictable.

The phone rang. Zach was grateful for the interruption.

"A new one," said the voice on the other end. "Fifteen years old. I'm sending you the data now."

Zach opened his e-mail and studied the statistics. He could've left the interview to someone else, but he needed to get away from Julianne for a little while and let things settle down.

He went to his bedroom to grab the bag he always kept packed. Julianne was just getting out of bed. He got a good look at her in her black lace bra and panties. Great. Like he needed *that* image to carry with him.

She grabbed her sweater and held it to her chest.

He walked past her. "I have to leave."

"For how long?"

"A day or two." He went into the closet and stopped, giving her time to get dressed. He slid his hand across his abdomen. He'd wanted before, needed before, but not like this. She was different from any other woman he'd been attracted to. Wasn't his type at all. But…

He grabbed his suitcase. She was standing in the same spot when he emerged but was dressed. Just leave the room, he told himself. Go. Now. Keep walking.

Then he was standing in front of her, his suitcase on the floor, and he was kissing her, like a knight going off into battle. After a couple of seconds she was kissing him back, and he indulged himself in her warmth and passion, a memory to recall when he needed to.

"Be safe," she whispered against his mouth. "Come home."

He kissed her hard one more time then left without looking back, not wanting to see worry in her eyes. His part of the rescue wasn't dangerous, but for some reason he didn't want to tell her that. He kind of liked that she was worried.

Just what did that say about him?

Eleven

Julianne was bored and lonely, a lethal combination. Zach had been gone for two days. He'd called her a couple of times, keeping up the happy-marriage appearances for the Moodys, she assumed. She'd visited Lil, polished furniture, practiced the piano, watched movies and went for walks with the dogs.

At night she wallowed in Zach's bed but had been careful not to be nosy about his belongings, although she doubted he left anything around that he would care if she saw. His office door stayed locked.

The second night while getting ready for bed in the walk-in closet she heard a thump on the wall behind a rack of clothes. She froze. After a moment she hung up her pants and moved toward the wall. She pushed hangers aside, put her hand on the wall. Another thump.

She jerked her arm back and waited again. Nothing. She

gauged the size of the closet and realized it didn't take up all the space to the outside walls of the castle. She went into the hallway, walked it to the end. No door. No access of any kind to another room.

Returning to the bedroom she paced the distance from the door to the back wall of the closet. She looked for a secret panel, but found nothing. Then she paced off the distance in the hallway. Short by fifteen feet or so.

She realized then that the noises she'd heard from above while she was in the media room couldn't have been coming from the tower room, because it was on the third floor, or whatever that level would be called. The noises she'd heard had to have come from the space—a room?—nestled between Zach's bedroom and the outside wall.

She pressed an ear to the room-without-an-entrance, could just barely make out sounds. A television, maybe?

Julianne returned to the master bedroom, tugged on some warm clothes, grabbed a flashlight then made her way outside. She peered up at the castle and counted windows. An extra window for sure, next to the master bedroom.

And the light was on.

If she could get herself to higher ground she might be able to see inside. She looked around. The full moon was cloaked by dark clouds. The scent in the air indicated impending rain. She'd never walked the trails—if the narrow, winding paths could be called such—at night, without Zach. Would she get lost? Not if she kept the castle in sight.

Her stomach churned as she climbed, the beam from her flashlight bouncing along the uneven path. Every few seconds she turned to look at the castle. No movement. When she reached a level even with the second floor she sat on the cold, wet ground and waited.

There! Someone passed in front of the window again. A minute later the light in the tower room came on. Someone stood at the window looking out. Julianne was too far away to make out any details. The light from behind turned the person into a silhouette. Okay. It was starting to make sense. The woman who lived in the tower room also used the space below it. A suite, of sorts. Connected by an interior staircase most likely.

So, who was in there? In gothic novels a crazy relative often lived in the attic. It certainly wasn't any ghost, unless ghosts really could materialize. Had he or she chosen isolation…or been forced against their will?

Which was ridiculous. Of course Zach wasn't keeping anyone prisoner. Except…

She recalled the look on his face when she'd asked about Hannah, and he'd shown her a side of him she hadn't seen before, one that struck a little fear into her heart and had reminded her how little she knew him. She'd fantasized about him, turning him into her own ideal of a man, not the true picture.

Hannah. She'd only guessed there was a connection there. Many of her drawings were the view from the castle. A former girlfriend? Wife? Julianne realized she didn't even know if he'd been married before.

Was Hannah the person in the tower?

Julianne needed binoculars to see inside the secret rooms. She stood. Just as she did the light went off in the tower and, a minute later, in the room below. Julianne hadn't left a lamp on in the master bedroom. She had no guiding light to help her return.

A big, fat raindrop landed on Julianne's head, followed by another, then a whole lot more, then a deluge. She sprang up. She was already cold and wet from sitting on the ground. Now the freezing rain quickly drenched the rest of her.

Just keep moving downhill. You have to reach the bottom sometime.

She wished for lightning, anything to light up the surroundings and let her find her way, which became more obscured and confusing by the moment. She lost track of any semblance of a path as rain washed away dirt, carving tiny rivulets. She'd never seen rain this intense.

She got turned around. *Downhill.* The word repeated in her head as she got her bearings. *Downhill.* She fell, slipped while trying to stand up, fell again. She forced herself up and carefully made her way again.

Panic set in as she didn't reach a building or even level ground after hiking what seemed like far enough. The beam of her flashlight, while good enough to light a path ahead, didn't put out enough of a beacon through the downpour to illuminate anything more than thirty feet away.

Her stomach knotted. Her throat burned. Her hair was plastered to her head and face, a sopping mess, dripping into her clothes. *Zach! Find me. Come find me.*

Her silent plea went unanswered.

She slipped again, landing hard, knocking the wind out of her. She lay there, her eyes and mouth closed to the rainfall, unable to draw enough air to fill her lungs again. She rolled to her side, then her stomach, raised up on hands and knees, sucked in air, clawed at mud, slipped…

Something shoved her. She screamed, scrambled to find a foothold, then realized it was the dogs. She dropped to her knees, an arm around each neck and cried in relief.

"Take…me…home," she said breathlessly, hoping they

would understand, not sure they would respond to anyone's command other than Zach's.

She slipped a hand under each of their collars. "Home. Please."

They headed to the left, when she would've gone right, but she trusted them. At least she could sleep with them and stay warm. If they stayed with her.

Holding on to the dogs helped her keep her balance. How far had she gotten from the castle? It seemed to be taking forever to get back.

Two short whistles rang out. Zach? Instead of taking off, Archie barked…and barked and barked. Belle chimed in. They stopped walking, holding her in place, as well. The whistles came again. The barking alert started again in earnest. The beam of a powerful flashlight lit the trees around her.

"Here!" she called.

"Julianne?"

"Yes! Here!" She plopped to the ground. It *was* Zach. He was home. He would help her.

She went blind from the light he shined on her face. She wanted him to drop down beside her, to hold her, shelter her, tell her she was fine.

"What the hell are you doing?" he asked, no sympathy in his voice at all. The dogs greeted him. He patted them, praised them.

"I got lost," she said. "You're home." She sounded pathetic, but she didn't feel strong at the moment.

"What were you doing out?"

"I…couldn't sleep." Which was true. She wouldn't have been able to until she knew for sure about the room next to the master suite, and that a person lived in it.

He grabbed her hands and pulled her up. The dogs led the way. She discovered she was only about fifty feet from the castle. Almost home. If he hadn't arrived when he had, he never would've known about her foolish adventure. And the dogs would never have told.

The thought made her laugh, hysteria layering the sound. She cursed her father and brother for never letting her out in the world, therefore limiting her life skills. She should've been able to handle what had happened just fine on her own. Instead she'd fallen apart when Zach came to the rescue, making her seem even more immature than he already thought.

"You are the most idiotically reckless woman I've ever known," he muttered as they stood inside the utility room off the back entrance. He peeled off her coat as he talked, his movements jerky, fury in his voice and actions. "You didn't think you could fall down and hurt yourself and that no one would know until morning? You didn't realize you could slip off the edge of the cliff straight down to the rocks below, especially when it's muddy? You could've died! Do you understand that?"

"I'm s-sorry." Her teeth chattered.

He continued to undress her to her underwear. "You should be." He opened the laundry room door, reached inside and came back with a towel, which he held open, blocking his view. "Strip."

She decided not to argue. She'd been wrong to go out at night. She didn't want to upset him more than he was. So she stripped off her bra and panties and let him wrap her in the towel.

"Go take a hot shower," he said. "I'll be up soon."

She hurried away, toward the sanctuary of the shower.

The worst hadn't happened. She hadn't gotten lost or hurt herself, except her pride.

Yes, it could've been worse. Much worse.

She wanted to force the issue of who lived in the tower room but knew it wasn't the best time for questions of any kind.

She jogged up the stairs, went straight into the shower, planning to stay there until her bones warmed and she'd improved her story about why she'd been outside in the first place.

Zach draped Julianne's muddy clothes over a rack in the laundry room, then added his own. When he thought about the possibilities of what could've happened to her…

He'd come home, crept into their bedroom in the dark, not wanting to wake her, then discovered she wasn't in bed or even in the house. He'd called the dogs, commanded them to find her. They had. He might have been out there all night trying to track her in the rain.

All because she was having trouble sleeping.

He whipped a towel around himself, tucked it at the waist. The laundry room door opened.

"Mr. Zach," Mr. Moody said in surprise. "I didn't know you were home."

"I didn't need anything, so I decided not to wake you. Julianne was out in the storm, however."

The older man came to attention. "I didn't know…"

"I realize that. You would've hunted her down yourself. No harm came to her, but it can't happen again."

"I'll be more vigilant when you're not home."

"Thanks." She'd been entrusted by Jamey into his care. Zach had already taken advantage of that trust by kissing her, by almost making love to her. He couldn't let her be hurt—or worse. "I'm fairly certain she won't go out at night again."

"Got lost, did she?"

"I think she panicked."

"And the reason for her adventure?"

"She couldn't sleep."

Mr. Moody's brows lifted. "You believe it?"

"There's more, I'm sure. She has asked me about Hannah."

"Sir?"

"I was shocked, too. I don't know how she knows or how much, but she's got the name."

"I didn't say any—"

Zach cut him off with a gesture. "I'm sure of that. And of Mrs. Moody's silence on the subject."

"Lil?"

"I can't imagine it." No, not Lil. She was the only other person on the Prom who knew Hannah personally.

"There's no one else." Mr. Moody hesitated. "Except your friend Jamey."

"Not Jamey." He said the words with the certainty of his belief.

"Not intentionally."

"Not even by accident." Zach angled his head to look at the ceiling. "I think my wife awaits."

"You haven't had much of a honeymoon."

If you only knew. "Some things take precedence."

"Yes, I know. And a lot of us are grateful for that. For your sacrifices and now Julianne's."

Zach patted his shoulder and left the room, wishing he'd earned Mr. Moody's gratitude but knowing he'd failed. That Mr. and Mrs. Moody stuck with him was a testament to something, but Zach wasn't sure what.

He expected Julianne to be asleep by the time he got into bed. He didn't speak to her as he walked around the bed, into the bathroom and climbed in the shower.

What was he going to do about her curiosity, which had resulted in recklessness this time? Jamey would've killed him if—

No. Zach couldn't use Jamey as an excuse. He wouldn't have forgiven himself if something had happened to her. Not because she was his charge, but because she lived. And he cared about her.

There. He'd admitted it. It wasn't just physical attraction. She made him laugh. She teased and flirted with him. He liked her. He would miss her when she left. For the little bit of time he'd feared something horrible had happened to her, he'd come as close to panic as he'd known for a long time.

A few minutes later he left the bathroom and made his way to bed. She lay far, far away. Her breathing indicated she wasn't asleep.

"Don't ever do that again," he said more harshly than he'd intended when he was under the blankets.

"I can't promise you that."

He was proud of the fact he didn't groan, loud and long. "Julianne—"

"Zach." She turned toward him. "A situation may come up where I have to do that again."

"Like what?"

"I don't know. How would I know? But it may. I don't want to break a promise. But I'll tell you that I would only do it if I found myself without options."

He couldn't handcuff her completely. "Fair enough."

"Did you drive the boat in this rain?"

"I rented one. It'll be picked up tomorrow. How'd you pass the time while I was gone?"

"Slowly."

He smiled at the ceiling.

"Why do you do it, Zach?"

"Do what?"

"Rescue people."

"Someone needs to."

"I thought kidnap was the FBI's jurisdiction."

"It is."

"Do you work for them?"

"I used to." He could hear her interest pique. The bed shook a little as she rolled to her side.

"You quit?"

"A few years ago."

"Why?"

"I found bureaucracy too…restrictive."

"Meaning you're a rule breaker, and you couldn't break rules?"

"Something like that. By the book doesn't always work."

"So you quit, formed your own team and wrote your own book."

"That sums it up."

"Have you been happy with that decision, Zach?"

"I've never looked back."

"And you break laws in your pursuit of retrieving people who are kidnapped."

"Not necessarily breaking laws all the time but being willing to take risks outside of the manual."

"Which brings me back to my original question. Why do you do it?"

"And my original answer. Because someone needs to."

"Where you went this time—were you successful?"

"Yes." Just barely. The boy was almost killed. But he wasn't, Zach reminded himself. He wasn't.

"Do things usually happen that quickly?"

"The first forty-eight hours are the critical window." She'd asked and he'd answered enough for one night. "Good night, Julianne."

After about ten seconds of silence she also said good-night.

Later, when he was still struggling to sleep, he felt her come toward him, the bed barely moving, the sheets barely rustling. She stopped just short of touching him. He waited a few minutes then he slipped an arm around her sleepily and pulled her close. She pressed her face against his neck and sighed.

It was too damn bad she fit there so perfectly.

Twelve

Later that night Julianne woke up cold and alone. She opened her eyes, seeking Zach, missing the heat of his body. He was gone, had been gone for a while, if the cold sheets were any indication. She lifted her head, looked at the clock. Almost 3:00 a.m.

Where was he? She hadn't heard the phone ring. The bathroom light wasn't on. She could hear voices, though, faint and distant.

She shoved the comforter aside, got out of bed and crept to the closet. She pressed her ear to the wall adjoining the secret room. Nothing. But when she left the closet, the sound of the voices increased, not to a comprehendible volume but enough to verify she wasn't crazy. She did hear voices—which seemed to be coming from behind a painting on the wall.

Her pulse pounding, she tilted the painting and discovered a hole in the wall, a pipe from which the voices became distinguishable.

"You knew it couldn't go on forever," Zach said.

"Why not?" a woman answered. "You promised you would take care of me."

Julianne pressed a hand to her mouth.

"I never expected you to stay this long. I assumed that at some point you would want something different."

"I want to stay with *you*."

"I'm married now. I told you that. Things have changed."

"I don't see why I have to change because of it."

"I'm tired of the deception. Julianne has already figured out that someone is living in the tower. She's not naive enough to believe it's a ghost. And I wouldn't put it past her to find the key and let herself in. She's resourceful *and* a free spirit. It's a problematic combination."

What did that mean? Julianne wondered, frowning at the wall. She was problematic?

"I don't want to meet her."

"You've made that clear."

"You promised me I'd always be your girl."

"You still are, Hannah. That won't change."

Hannah. Julianne flattened her back to the cold wall and closed her eyes. Hannah lived in the tower room.

"I'm not ready," Hannah said.

"At least meet Julianne. You'd like her."

"I hate her."

A long silence followed, some kind of stand-off, Julianne guessed. Two strong-willed people, neither willing to back down.

"Go to bed," he said, resignation in his voice. "Get some sleep."

Julianne stood frozen for a few seconds trying to digest what she'd overheard. Then she scrambled to realign the painting and get back into bed before Zach returned.

Her heart pounded, stealing her ability to hear. She curled in a ball, her back facing his side of the bed. She could barely breathe, there was so much pressure on her chest. Hannah. In the tower room. Locked in. Someone who meant a lot to Zach—or at least *had* meant a lot. Their current relationship wasn't clear, except that Zach wanted Hannah to move on, and she didn't want to. Nor did she want him out of her life. Where did that leave Julianne? Who mattered more to him?

The thought of sharing him…

The bed jostled under Zach's weight. She hadn't even heard the door open. He seemed to be staring at her, maybe wondering why she'd moved so far on the other side of the bed?

He moved closer, tucked himself behind her. His arm slipped around her waist. Tears sprang to her eyes. She was weak, wanting him as she did when another woman also had some sort of claim on him, someone he had an emotional past with. He only had a convenient future with Julianne, not until death do us part, but until the coast was clear.

His fingers grazed her stomach through her pajama top, softly, steadily. He slipped his hand under the fabric and stroked her skin.

"You're awake," he whispered.

"No. I'm dreaming."

She felt him smile where his lips touched her shoulder. Did she want this to happen? Yes. *Yes.* She wanted him. But with all the secrets that hung between them? Was she just a substitute for Hannah? Could he be that dishonest? He'd seemed to have a high degree of integrity and selflessness.

She'd long harbored a fantasy of finding the perfect man and falling in love, with no secrets between them, nothing hidden from the other. After an entire life of secrecy, she needed that kind of relationship.

But, oh, how she wanted him. She knew she couldn't keep enduring night after night sleeping beside him and not make love with him.

"Is this okay?" he asked, cupping her breast.

"Yes," she answered, making her decision. She didn't want to miss out on something so glorious, so exciting. She arched her back as he stroked her, teased her, drew her nipples into hard, aching knots. Heat gathered between her legs and spread up her body. Needing to kiss him, she turned and found his mouth with hers. He cupped her head, slowing the pace, taking control. She shook.

"Relax," he said against her lips. "Just let it happen."

She dug her fingers into his back. "I can't. I want…"

"So do I. But let's make this memorable."

He spent a lot of time getting acquainted with her mouth, seemingly not in a hurry to move things along with any speed. She appreciated the time he took, the way he nibbled and tasted and savored, at the same time managing to peel off her pajamas, and his T-shirt and sweatpants, then they were skin to skin. Still he only kissed her until she finally pulled his hand down to her breast.

"Please," she whispered.

He indulged her, caressing her, dipping low to take her nipple in his mouth, drawing it into his warmth and wetness. His tongue performed magic. She lifted toward him even more. He let his hand drift down her abdomen until his fingers settled on her with an exquisite intimacy. She tipped back her head and moaned as he stroked and dipped and explored.

She reached for him, too, grabbing hold, enjoying the strength and heat until he wrapped a hand around her wrist, stopping her.

"Not a good idea," he said.

She pulled away reluctantly. He'd felt so good, so vital. She wanted to feel him inside her, where he belonged. She wanted to know what it felt like. Still he was in no hurry but did things to her that emptied her mind of everything but the touch of his lips and tongue and fingers. Pressure built, a kind of yearning that defied description, a need for satisfaction. Completion. Merger.

Mating.

Need spiraled through her. Hunger had her begging. When he moved over her, she wrapped her legs around him. He positioned himself. She felt the tip of him press forward, slowly, gently. "Okay?" he asked every few seconds. After a while her body's demands took away her ability to speak. In her mind she heard *yes* over and over. *Like that. Oh, that feels so good.*

But what came out of her mouth were groans and nonsense sounds. Reaction, response. Joy. His arms clamped around her just as the pain struck, piercing, fleeting. Done with. Sore, maybe, but still the building pressure, the building ecstasy. Then a shattering explosion from deep inside, spreading everywhere. His mouth on hers, hard, demanding, hot. Her fingernails in his back, holding on. His body sliding against hers, rhythmic, possessive. Then the slowing down, catching of breath, finding earth. Peace and happiness and wonder.

She wrapped her arms around him, keeping him close.

Her eyes welled. It had been beautiful, awesome and memorable, as he'd known was right for both of them. She replayed it over and over in her head, imprinting it, all of it—touch, sound, smell, sight, taste.

"Okay?" he asked.

She nodded.

"Did I hurt you?"

She nodded.

"I'm sorry."

"A good pain, Zach. Really good."

"No regrets?"

"None." She realized he needed to hear that it had been good for her. She had nothing to compare it with, but she gave him the words, anyway. "You made it special. I won't forget it ever."

He rolled them onto their sides, keeping their legs entwined. He kissed her gently, brushed her hair from her face.

"Why tonight?" she asked. *Tell me the truth.*

"I realized you were right."

"About what?"

"That this marriage may last for quite a while. And if you were willing to make it physical, knowing it will come to an end, then so was I. Selfish, I guess."

She needed time to think about what he'd said and how he'd said it. He hadn't hesitated in his response, which meant he'd thought about it. He had needs and she was convenient? Was she willing to settle for that?

And what about Hannah?

"I'll be right back," he said, giving her a gentle kiss.

At some point he'd put on a condom. She was grateful for that. Her plans didn't include a baby at this point. Of course, her plans hadn't included marriage, either. *Life is what happens while you're making plans.* Where had she heard that?

He returned with a warm, wet washcloth and bathed her. She was glad the lights were off, as the intimacy of his actions heated her face.

"You sure you're okay?" he asked.

"I'm sure."

"You're very quiet."

"It's not every day a woman loses her virginity."

"To her husband, as you pointed out."

"I think that's probably especially unusual." Did he feel proprietary about her because of it? "Zach?"

"What?"

"We don't need to talk this to death, you know. It happened. I was willing. I don't expect anything different from you."

"Don't you?"

Something about the inflection in his voice alerted her. Was he arguing the point?

"You don't think you have a right to something different from me?" he continued.

"I'm not sure what you mean." She was trying to be sophisticated, even if she didn't feel that way. Truth was, she didn't think he wanted her to fall in love with him, that it would complicate things too much.

He didn't explain what he meant. After a minute he got out of bed. She heard water run in the bathroom then he came back and drew her close.

"We'll talk about it another time," he said, his breath warm against her face. Then he tucked her more tightly against him. She slipped an arm around him. She wanted to cry. Why did she want to cry? He'd been tender and kind and selfless. What did she have to complain about?

You don't trust him. Not completely.

The words lit up like neon in her mind. She would've trusted him, blindly, if she hadn't been aware of Hannah's existence. How old was she? What did she look like? Why was she choosing to stay on the island? In the tower? Isolated?

The questions drifted away as her body demanded sleep.

"Good night," he whispered.

"Night." That was the last thing she remembered until morning when she woke up to an empty bed. She stretched, recalled she was naked and why.

She was glad he wasn't there to see her face flush as she relived what had happened between them. She smiled at the ceiling. Then she remembered the conversation between Zach and Hannah.

Julianne glanced at the painting on the wall, the one that hid the listening pipe. The smile left her face as she realized there was a matching painting on the opposite wall. She stared at it. Wondered.

Had to know.

She climbed out of bed, walked warily to the painting and shoved it to one side. Not just matching paintings. Matching listening holes. And she would bet anything it led to the tower room she'd been assigned to.

The bedroom door opened. Zach.

"You spied on me."

"Julianne—"

"You listened to my conversations on the phone with Jamey. You knew I'd asked him to help me leave." She remembered something else. "You heard me tell him I missed my mochas. You had Mrs. Moody bring them. It wasn't her idea at all. You heard whatever I said to myself.

I had no privacy whatsoever." She let the painting fall into place and turned around. Her fury was complicated by the fact she was also naked, and therefore feeling more vulnerable than ever in her life.

Expressionless, he walked past her into the bathroom and returned with a robe, his robe. She grabbed it from him, not letting him help her don it.

"You had privacy, Julianne. I admit I overheard things a couple of times, but it was rare that I intruded."

"Once is too much."

He hesitated. "Yes. You're right."

After a moment she strode across the room and lifted the mate. "And this one?"

He crossed his arms.

"Hannah has no privacy, either," she said.

"Nor from you, either, apparently," he replied, the angles of his face sharpening. "Get dressed."

"I don't take orders—"

"Get dressed, *please*, Julianne. I'll take you to meet Hannah."

"She doesn't want to meet me."

He stared at her. "It's time to end that secret." He walked away. "I'll be back in fifteen minutes."

The door shut with a quiet but final click.

"*Thirty* minutes!" she shouted at the door, not letting him have the upper hand.

"Okay!" he called back.

Her lips twitched. She refused to let it become a smile. If he wanted her to meet Hannah against her will, it meant he was placing Julianne's needs first.

That made her happy.

Thirteen

Zach prepared for any possible reaction from Hannah. She might scream or clam up or run off to her downstairs room and lock herself in. No matter what she did, however, Julianne would know the truth. That much he'd decided.

He led the way up the tower stairs, Julianne behind him. He didn't know what she knew about Hannah, how much was speculation and how much was fact. That she'd overheard a conversation between him and Hannah was obvious.

He knocked on the door. Julianne's nerves were apparent in her ragged breathing. Tension seeped from her and wrapped around him.

Hannah opened the door, spotted Julianne on the step below him and started to slam the door. He blocked the move.

"I told you I didn't want to meet her! Go away. Go away now." She hurried off. He caught up with her before she could descend the spiral staircase into her bedroom on the level below.

"Please stay," he said, although not giving her an opportunity to do otherwise. He was aware of Julianne coming into the room hesitantly. "Hannah, this is my wife, Julianne. Julianne, this is Hannah, my sister."

Zach gave Julianne credit. Her reaction wouldn't be obvious to anyone not looking for it. She hadn't known Hannah was his sister. Had she thought he was keeping a lover in the tower?

"I'm very happy to meet you," Julianne said, approaching but not getting too close. "I've seen your drawings. You're a wonderful artist."

Hannah crossed her arms. "How old are you?"

"Twenty-three."

"Same as you," Zach said, realizing how childlike Hannah was when compared to Julianne, at the same age.

"And you're already married," Hannah said with a sniff.

Julianne smiled. "So it seems."

Zach almost laughed.

"I've never had a boyfriend. I've been…here."

"I think you'll find we have a lot in common," Julianne said.

Zach appreciated that she remained calm, her voice reassuring. He saw Hannah respond to Julianne's nonthreatening manner. Hannah was taller and more slender, her hair straight and slightly more blond than Julianne's. On the surface they were different, but Julianne was right. They shared some similarities.

He let go of his sister, deciding she wouldn't bolt. After a moment, she walked to Julianne and put out her hand.

"Welcome to the family, dysfunctional as it is."

Julianne gave no obvious reaction to Hannah's severe limp. She ignored the extended hand and hugged his sister instead. "Thank you. I'm glad to have a sister. And I doubt yours is any more dysfunctional than mine."

Hannah's discomfort at the hug didn't seem to faze Julianne, who smiled widely as she released Hannah.

"Have you had breakfast?" Julianne asked.

"Hours ago."

"Would you like to come down to the dining room and sit with me while I eat?"

Hannah's back stiffened. "I have work to do."

"Okay. Maybe another time."

"Maybe."

"May I come back to visit, Hannah?"

"I guess so. Make sure you knock."

"I will. I'm so glad we met."

Julianne left. Zach studied his sister, whose face flushed.

"Okay, so I like her okay," she muttered. "Don't think things are going to change because of it."

"It's always been your decision."

"Okay. Just so we're clear."

He hugged her, something he hadn't done in a long time. His throat burned. He could see a future for her now. Maybe not right away, but sooner than he would've imagined yesterday.

Jamey had sent him the best gift possible when he'd sent Julianne. He'd thought it would be temporary, but the after-effects would be far -reaching.

Now instead of Zach having repaid Jamey by taking Julianne in, he was going to owe him again.

* * *

"I don't understand why you couldn't tell me about Hannah," Julianne said to Zach in bed that night. "What was the big secret?"

They were lying on their sides, one small lamp giving the room a little bit of light. She was enjoying how he trailed his fingers down her arm, caressing and teasing.

"That was her choice, not mine. Except for Lil and the Moodys, you're the only person on the island to meet her, although others know about her."

"But why?"

"Hannah has a lot of emotional scars that run very deep. For a while after we moved here she would leave the castle to do her drawings. She met Lil by accident that way and they became friends. But Hannah became increasingly, I don't know, angry? Belligerent? Hostile? More reclusive, too. She stopped coming out of her room. For a while Lil could visit Hannah in her room, but even that changed. I'm very worried about her."

His hand settled on Julianne's arm, no longer teasing.

"She usually takes care of the children we rescue. That night when we brought Jacob here, she'd taken medication because her hip was hurting, or so she said. She knew Jacob would be arriving, yet she'd taken a pill that would make it impossible for her to stay awake and care for him. She loves kids. I don't know why she did it. And now she seems afraid of everything."

"And you don't have a clue why?"

"No. None. Maybe I've kept her too safe. Maybe I've prevented her from becoming an independent adult. I've sheltered her."

"Why have you? What happened to her that you feel the need to do that?"

He didn't answer for a long time. She waited, hoping, but prepared to have him change the subject.

"Hannah was kidnapped when she was ten."

"Oh, no!" Julianne gripped his arm.

"So was I. I was seventeen. And our brother, Marshall. He was seven."

"Zach." Her heart opened to him, to the unmasked pain in his voice. "What happened?"

He rolled onto his back and stared at the ceiling. "Our parents died when Marsh was very young, almost two. We were sent to live with our grandparents, my father's parents. They were—are—extremely wealthy. Family's been in San Francisco since the gold rush. They were…uninvolved with us. Very distant. It wasn't a warm household, but we had each other."

"You were the big brother and dad and protector."

He nodded.

"What happened?"

"We were being driven home from school, a private school, when our driver's door was pulled open by a man wearing a ski mask. Another one climbed in back with us. The driver was dragged out, shot and left for dead. We were blindfolded and driven for hours to a cabin in the Sierras. It was winter, and the snow was ten feet deep. We were dragged into a basement and left there."

"For how long?"

"Days. Food was tossed in. There was a bathroom attached, so we had water, although only cold water. We were guarded by only one man and he would barely speak to us." Zach sat up, his gaze on the far wall. "Marsh was asthmatic, and he'd almost used up his inhaler, because he was so stressed he'd had to use it more often. I begged for another one and was told to deal with it. There was no way to *deal* with it. If we'd had hot water, it could've helped. Steam could've helped."

She waited in silence for him to continue

He looked over his shoulder at her. "I figured out a way to escape through an incredibly small window, blocked by snow. I would have to dig my way up out of it, and I figured I only had about six hours—the time between our guard's last visit at night and first one in the morning.

"I also knew I couldn't take Marsh and Hannah along. I didn't know where we were, how far away from civilization, how far of a walk to find help, which direction to go. None of us wore clothes suited to the weather. There was no way he could survive that kind of trip. And if I left him alone, I wasn't sure he would survive. I knew he would panic if the guard showed up before I returned. And what if I couldn't find my way back? I didn't know whether to go or stay. I needed to protect them. I also needed to save them."

Zach rubbed his face. Julianne wanted to hold him. The sadness that weighed him down, that registered in his face and voice and posture, brought tears to her eyes.

"But Hannah said I had to go, that it was our only chance. Marsh agreed." He paused again, as if reliving it. "It took me four hours to dig out. The snow at the base was so hard I had to carve it out with a spoon, but I could also carve footholds in, too. Then as I got higher the snow was fresher and falling in on me from all sides."

"You could've been buried alive." The thought of him struggling to save his brother and sister, of digging and digging and digging, almost without hope, infuriated her.

"It was a risk. But I finally got above the snow and took off running. When I eventually came to a plowed road more than an hour later, I flagged down the first car. I wasn't sure anyone would stop. I looked like a frozen wild man, I'm sure. But it was Jamey. And Jamey would never pass by someone who needed help."

Julianne gasped. "What was he doing there?"

"Driving home from Lake Tahoe. He was a bounty hunter in those days. He had a gun. But he also knew it was too risky to go in there alone. We marked the place and went to the nearest house and called the police. Everything went wrong. Everything." He seemed to get more rigid. "Our guard saw them coming. He used Marsh as a shield, and he couldn't take the stress. He went into acute respiratory failure and he died."

Tears slipped down Julianne's cheeks. She put a hand on his back, gently, cautiously. He didn't slough it off.

"The bastard shoved Hannah down a flight of stairs. Her leg and pelvis were shattered. The growth plate was broken. That's why she limps now. Physically she recovered, except for the limp, but not mentally. We had a psychiatrist literally living at the house for months."

"Wasn't there ransom demanded for all of you?"

He snorted. "My grandparents decided to try to negotiate the ransom on their own, without calling the FBI. That's what stalled the rescue attempt."

"Why did they do that?"

"So there wouldn't be a scandal."

"Zach. How could you even look them in the eye?"

"I couldn't. As far as I was concerned, they had killed Marsh. They had damaged Hannah."

"And you."

"I was old enough to deal with it."

She didn't believe that, not for a second. But if it helped him to cope with the guilt and pain, so be it.

"I left home on my eighteenth birthday. I was determined to become an FBI agent, thinking that my experience would make the difference. I would work my way into a position where I had authority, and kidnap rescues would be my specialty. No one else would die."

"But you found yourself tied by rules that prevented you from succeeding."

He said nothing for what seemed like forever. Deciding whether to confide more? She didn't know. She simply waited.

"I was an agent for four years," he said at last, "when we got a case involving a thirteen-year-old boy. Similar M.O. Son of wealthy parents, snatched on the way home from the same private school. Except this time, the parents called the FBI right away. We tracked them to a remote location. I wanted to surprise the bastard, make my way inside, just me. I thought if anyone else went along, he would see. I knew I could get in. But I was ordered to to stand down. We followed procedure and surrounded the cabin. Called to him on a loudspeaker. The bastard was a lunatic. He decided on murder-suicide instead of giving himself up. The boy died." He paused. "His name was Christopher Moody."

It was like a stab in the heart. She would never feel sorry for herself again. Compared to what Zach and Hannah and the Moodys had endured, she'd lived the life of a princess.

Suddenly her plans seemed frivolous. So she'd been denied the right to attend college, to live on her own, to be free to live independently. What did it matter?

"I failed to bring their son home. I knew I couldn't let

that happen again. By then I'd gathered a number of resources. I quit the FBI and put together a team of former
agents and others who were willing to risk their lives for
strangers. They're spread all over the country. They report
kidnappings to me from their sources, which is usually
someone in law enforcement who knows we do things differently, faster, for one thing. Our rescue rate is higher
than when everything is done by the book."

"What's your role?"

"My trust fund, and half of Marsh's, came to me when
I turned twenty-five. I can't think of a better use for it than
to finance this venture, plus I'm central operations. Without
someone to oversee everything…"

She wondered if he was trying to justify his lack of
physical involvement in the rescues. "Your job would be
impossible to replace, Zach. Everyone knows you're the
one to contact, right? You're the mastermind."

"If not me, then someone else would step up."

Okay, he didn't want to be complimented. He was
driven to do what he did. Praise wasn't part of the deal.
Only success was.

"I've seen your wall of photos. You've helped so
many people."

"You've seen the other wall, too. Every failure is one
too many."

"I'm so sorry for the Moodys."

He shoved his fingers through his hair, as if tired of remembering. "They'd had Christopher very late in life, after
having given up on ever conceiving. He was everything. They
had no desire to return to their old life. When they heard what
I was doing, they begged me to let them come here. I couldn't
save their son, but they wanted to help me save others."

"And Lil and Misery and all the rest of the people on this island?"

"Most of them came as the result of contact with me and my team, whether a success or failure. They grieve here. Some move on. Many have stayed. But it's their decision whether to talk about it."

There was a caution in his voice and she responded to it. "I won't bring it up, I promise." She moved so that she could face him. "What can I do for you? How can I help?"

"I would appreciate anything you can do to bring Hannah back into the world. When I compared her to you, I realized how out of touch she is. She only sees life through television and books. She's afraid of something, but I don't know what. She's forgotten how not to be afraid. Maybe she never knew. But for a while, I thought she was making a breakthrough."

"So this is kind of the blind leading the blind," Julianne said, teasing gently. "One sheltered girl to another."

"You're much more worldly."

"I can see that. I'm not a psychiatrist, though, Zach."

"No. You would be a friend. I think that's what she needs. What she missed out on for thirteen years."

"I'll do my best."

He slid a hand behind her neck and tugged her to him, kissing her hard, then dragging her against his chest, enveloping her in his arms. "I'll bet you had no idea what you were in for when you arrived on the Prom."

"You'd win that bet." She listened to his heartbeat, strong and steady. "Is it okay if the Moodys know I know?"

"I think they'll take one look at your sympathetic face and know that you know. I'll tell them. They've come to like you a lot."

"Goes both ways." She settled against him and closed

her eyes, suddenly fighting tears. She felt so sorry for him, for all of them. And so angry at the cruelty of other people.

He pressed a kiss to her head. "What's wrong?"

"Nothing."

"Something."

"Just feeling sad for you."

"You could make me feel better."

"How?"

"Do you really have to ask, Julianne?"

She understood that he needed to stop thinking about the past. She sat up, placed her palms against his bare stomach and let them slide to the waistband of his boxer shorts. "Am I getting warm?"

He sucked in a breath. "Warm."

She slipped a hand under the waistband.

"Warmer," he said.

She wrapped her hand around him and felt his strong response, flattered that she could do that, and so quickly.

"Hot."

"Yeah," she whispered, angling her head for a kiss. "Scorching."

"Are you sore?"

"I don't know. Why don't we find out?"

She was sore, but not enough to give up the chance to make love with him again. She didn't know how much time they had. The time would come soon enough when she would have to...*get* to leave. She couldn't stay there. She would go crazy.

But for now, he was hers and she was his. And that would have to do.

Fourteen

"So your name is Venus? Really?" Hannah asked Julianne a few days later, then she giggled. "That's weird."

"I've taken a lot of teasing." Julianne held her pose, seated in a chair in front of the tower window while Hannah sketched her portrait.

"Why are you calling yourself Julianne?"

"It's my new identity. I didn't change my last name because Johnson is common enough to protect me."

Hannah stopped drawing, her interest piqued. "Protect you from what?"

"From having to testify against my brother. He's in jail."

"For what?"

"Extortion, among other things."

"Extortion?" Her expression was one of shock and curiosity. "Did you run away?"

"Kind of. I gave a deposition, but the prosecutor thought

my testimony wouldn't be necessary. I didn't really know much about Nico's business." Julianne rolled her head. "I'm cramping."

"Why didn't you say so? Take a break." Hannah set aside her pad and pen. "I don't understand why you had to run away."

"Because my brother isn't the only person involved. He's part of a...group."

"A mob?" Hannah's eyes widened.

Julianne shrugged. She didn't know what to call it. "Anyway, they would want to make sure I don't testify, because they know I wouldn't lie. So we decided I shouldn't be where they could find me and take me or something."

"You mean they would kill you?"

"No." She didn't know that for sure. It seemed too extreme, however. "But they would keep me hidden. I can't go through that again. Plus I'm sick and tired of someone telling me what to do."

"But now you have Zach to protect you."

Julianne clenched her teeth. She'd almost slipped up. Hannah didn't know their marriage wasn't going to be forever. Julianne had gotten so comfortable with his sister that she hadn't been thinking about her plan and how she would leave as soon as she could. The reminder had come at the right time.

"Yes, I have Zach now," she said, then stood. "Can we finish later? Mr. Moody is taking me to Orcas to do some Christmas shopping. Want to come?"

Hannah hesitated, which Julianne took as a good sign. "No, thanks."

"Only five days to Christmas."

"I'm done with my shopping."

"Will you help decorate the tree?"

"We're having a tree?"

Julianne had just assumed so. "You don't usually?"

"Not since— Not for a couple of years."

What had Hannah been about to say? Not since she'd barricaded herself in her room?

"Where do you put your presents?" Julianne asked.

"Everyone comes to my room. We don't do much to celebrate. Julianne?"

She had started for the door but stopped and turned around. "What?"

"You never mention your parents."

Julianne looked past Hannah at the view out her window. "My father died ten years ago. My mother abandoned us when I was little." It never got easier to say.

"She left you? I didn't know mothers…did that."

Julianne couldn't come up with a quick response. She hated her mother for leaving her with her father, for thinking only of herself. "I don't care anymore."

"Well, I'm sorry. At least I had Zach."

Julianne's throat burned at the sympathy in Hannah's voice. "I'm sorry about your parents, too."

Hannah took a step toward Julianne, stopped, then came the rest of the way and hugged Julianne. It was the first time she'd initiated a hug. Julianne came close to crying.

They moved apart awkwardly.

"So," Hannah said, not making eye contact. "Being married and all—is kissing wonderful?"

Julianne laughed at the unexpected question. "No complaints here. You've never tried it, not even in high school?"

"I was homeschooled. No way to meet boys."

"You have some catching up to do." Julianne said the

words as casually as possible, as if it would be easy for Hannah to make her way in the world, when it wouldn't be. Even though it was what Julianne wanted to do, it wasn't going to be easy for her, either. Especially now that she'd seen how people suffered sometimes just to get through life. "I'll come see you when I get back."

She closed the door behind her. She'd been afraid a few times in her life, but not paralyzed by fear like Hannah.

Could Julianne lure Hannah out of her room? Into life? Was it too lofty a goal for someone who hardly had any life skills herself?

It would make Zach happy, and she wanted to do that.

Now, exactly how could she accomplish such a miracle?

Zach waited in his bedroom for Julianne to come say goodbye before she left for Orcas with Mr. Moody. She didn't, which surprised him. It also surprised him that it mattered so much.

She'd gotten under his skin. He didn't like it.

He was even envious—he refused to use the word *jealous*—of the amount of time Hannah spent with her. He should be happy that they were becoming friends. He *was* happy about that.

He'd felt guilty for years about having to leave Hannah behind when he left home. He couldn't take her to college with him, since she was only eleven, but also their grandparents had become more caring since the kidnapping and Marsh's death. When Hannah turned eighteen, Zach had asked her to live with him, but she'd turned him down, out of fear, he guessed—until he'd found the Prom, where she wouldn't have to go out in the world unless she chose to. She'd had no qualms about leaving home then, except for the trip itself. He'd rented a private plane to bring them to Anacordes, then she'd had her first—and last—boat ride to get to the island. She had barely said a word the whole trip, her fear at being out of her comfort zone evident and sad.

When her own trust fund matured in another two years, she wouldn't even be in the position of having to find a job to support herself. Financially he never had to work another day in his life, either, but the satisfaction he'd found from his work had kept him going, giving him little time to dwell on the past. His sister had too much time to dwell.

How could he get her off the island to experience life? After years and years of analysis, she still couldn't fend for herself. He knew he was enabling her, as her psychiatrist called it, by allowing her to stay in the tower, but what choice did he have? Throw her to the wolves?

He leaned against the wall next to a window and stared outside, wondering if it would rain. It would ruin Julianne's shopping trip, an excursion she'd been happy about. So happy she hadn't tracked him down to kiss him goodbye…

Zach shoved away from the wall. He was dwelling on Julianne because for once he had no work to do. He had two teams tracking the two victims whose pictures hung on his office wall. There was nothing more he could do. He went to his office anyway and realized there was something he *could* do.

He settled in at the computer, made a few phone calls, then met Julianne and Mr. Moody at the side door when they returned. It seemed the most natural thing in the world to take her in his arms and kiss her hello.

"I guess you missed me," she said, eyeing Mr. Moody, who was unloading packages from the Jeep.

He started to say he had when he noticed what stuck out the back of the Jeep. "You bought a Christmas tree."

"A little one."

He estimated it was at least eight feet tall. "I'm not sure our old lights still work. We don't have many ornaments either."

"So Mr. Moody told me. I bought lights. And we can make more decorations."

He couldn't picture himself sitting around the dining room table stringing popcorn and cranberries. "*We* meaning you and Hannah?"

"And you," she said with a grin, then pulled out more packages from the car after Mr. Moody went into the house. "A family affair, as Christmas should be."

"I'll supervise."

"And string the lights."

"I can do that." Her contagious enthusiasm boosted his spirits, that and what he planned to do next. "I have to leave town in a couple of days."

She stood with her arms full of bags. "Why?"

"Something I have to do. I'll be back for Christmas."

She stared at him. "You'll be safe?"

"Always."

"Don't make promises you can't keep. Not everything is within your control."

"You're right. In fact rarely is anything within my control. But this particular time, it is."

Mr. Moody returned, and Julianne went into the house. Zach helped unload the tree, then held it while the older man sawed an inch off the trunk base. Because Julianne had disappeared he helped set the tree in the base, then worked on the lights. It took him two hours and ten strands.

He'd just plugged in the lights when Julianne came downstairs for dinner.

"It's beautiful," she said, slipping an arm around his waist and leaning into him.

He kissed her head, ran his hand down her hair. "I'd forgotten what it was like to celebrate Christmas." Christmas with his grandparents had been formal and showy, their guest list for parties from among San Francisco's elite. He barely remembered the ones with his parents, even though he'd been twelve when they died. He only recalled being happy and surprised. He'd taken it for granted. And the only one they'd celebrated at the castle had been strained and awkward, as if none of them knew how to celebrate the holiday.

Wanting to stop the old family memories he kissed Julianne then, and she responded with an honesty that made him uneasy, considering the circumstances of their marriage. Then he forgot all about his reasons and deepened the kiss. She went up on tiptoe, wrapped her arms around his neck. Soft, throaty sounds of need rose from her. She tightened her hold. He ran his hands down her sides, cupped her waist, pulled her close. Urgency rose up in him.

He scooped her into his arms, headed for the staircase. "Hold dinner," he said to Mrs. Moody as she came into the hallway at the same time, carrying a tray. He felt Julianne tuck her face against his neck, as if embarrassed.

"Yes, sir." Laughter tinged Mrs. Moody's words.

He couldn't wait to get his wife in bed. She'd gotten more daring every night, her touch more confident, her desire more apparent. He kicked the bedroom door shut but didn't put her down until he reached the bed. He dropped her there, followed her down, blanketing her. Her legs wrapped around him, her hips arched to meet his. She sucked in a breath as he slipped his hands under her rear, then she released a long, low moan as he moved against her. He thought she was about to climax from the movement alone when she pushed at his shoulders.

"Roll over." Her voice registered husky and full of need. He did as she asked, gladly.

"I want to be in charge, okay?" she asked, her face flushed.

As if he would turn that down? "I'm yours," he answered.

She undressed him, her hands shaking, which filled him as much with tenderness as desire. She undressed herself, her hands shaking even more. Then she dragged her hands down his chest, his stomach, his abdomen, and beyond. Her fingers danced over him, feathery and fluttery, tickling and arousing. She bent over him, tasted him with her warm, wet tongue, something she hadn't done before…and he was lost. The innocence of her exploration turned him inside out. She took him in her hot, searching mouth…and he was found. Her desire to please him, her need to explore, her obvious pleasure at pleasuring him brought him a satisfaction he had never known.

He grabbed her head, keeping her there until he couldn't hold off it another second. He tried to stop her.

"Just enjoy it," she whispered, barely stopping.

He didn't need any convincing. Sensation coiled through and around him, sneaking under his skin, making slow, slithery moves downward, downward. He yielded to its power, gloried in its release. He went blind and deaf. There was only the feel of her mouth and hands, the vibration of her throaty moans transferring to his body, the scent of her perfume, distinctively Julianne…

Seconds, minutes or maybe hours later he settled against the mattress and opened his eyes. She was sitting on her heels watching him. Her eyes were suspiciously bright, her expression solemn. She was asking if she'd done okay without saying the words.

He pulled her into his arms. "That was amazing."

"Really?"

"Cross my heart." He began a tender assault on her, payback. He took his time, enjoying the heat of her kisses, the lushness of her breasts, the tautness of her nipples. Her skin was soft, smooth, kissable. He knelt between her legs, draping them over his thighs, and explored her. She never once opened her eyes.

"Tell me what you like," he ordered quietly.

"Everything." She raised her hips as he dragged his fingertips down her. "I like everything."

"This?" He bent down, ran his tongue along the same path. She squirmed. "Yes."

He slipped a finger inside her. "This?"

"Mmm-hmm."

"How about this?" He settled his mouth on her.

Only a garbled response reached his ears before she was arching high and calling his name, her body rigid for several long seconds, then she started to drift. He took her up again. She climaxed a second time, longer and louder. He rose above her, plunged into her, found paradise. He didn't try to be gentle. He couldn't be gentle. He wanted her, all of her. She dug her fingernails into his flesh, tipped back her head and matched his rhythm. She peaked. A moment later, he joined her.

It was only after they lay sprawled for several minutes, unable to move, barely able to breathe, that it struck him what he'd done.

He hadn't used a condom.

Fifteen

Julianne missed Zach. She tried not to. She didn't want to get more comfortable living on the Prom, but she didn't seem to have any willpower, especially in his bed, where she felt at ease. Too at ease. Too safe.

She smoothed the comforter with her hands then glanced at the clock. As of three minutes ago, it was officially Christmas.

Where was he?

He'd said he would be home for Christmas. Would he? He had called only once since he left, and sounded distant. In fact, ever since the last time they made love he'd been distant, not totally avoiding her, but not attentive, either. He hadn't made love to her again before he went away. What did that mean?

She jumped as the bedroom door opened, then she spotted Zach creeping in.

He's home. Her heart sighed. "I'm awake," she said, sitting up.

He came around the bed and sat, facing her. She slipped her hands into his and smiled. Could he see that in the dark?

"Merry Christmas," he said.

"Same to you." She snuggled against him. After a moment he wrapped his arms around her. "You're cold."

"I came across in the boat."

"Your boat? Did Mr. Moody come get you?"

He nodded, then brushed a hand through her hair. She closed her eyes, enjoying him, the scent of salt water on his skin and clothes, the underlying scent that was him and only him.

"Did you call earlier?" She hadn't heard the telephone ring.

"He has a separate line. How's Hannah?"

"Better every day, I think." Julianne leaned back to look at him in the dark. "I missed you."

His answer was to kiss her, but without his usual passion. The sweet tenderness of his lips against hers made her happy—and frustrated her. Something was going on with him.

Before she could ask what, she heard the dogs bark in a way she'd never heard before—frantic and threatening.

"Stay here," Zach ordered her then was out of the room before she'd fully registered the dogs' new sound, intensifying in volume and ferocity.

The dogs went wild. Julianne flew out of bed and raced to the window, flinging it open to the frigid night air. She couldn't see anything. The dogs continued to bark. A shot rang out. The barking stopped. Suddenly. Completely.

"Zach!" she screamed, frantic. *Noooo. No, no, no.*

She ran out of the room, raced down the stairs and along the hallway, her heart pounding, lungs burning. Into the dining room. The kitchen. The utility room— She skidded to a halt.

Mrs. Moody blocked the side door. "You can't go out there."

She tried to push her way past the older woman, who had become like an iron gate. "But, Zach—"

"You can't distract him."

Julianne clenched her teeth and looked for a way to get around the woman, who crossed her arms, looking even more immovable. "What's going on?"

"I don't know. An intruder of some sort or the dogs wouldn't have gone crazy like that."

"But they stopped…"

"I know." She glanced toward the door, fear in her eyes. "My husband is out there, too."

A sound of soft, hurried footsteps came from behind Julianne. She whirled around, a fleeting thought that Hannah had been drawn from her room, but a stranger approached, a dark-haired, fiftyish woman about Julianne's height, clutching her fleece robe at her throat, her eyes wide and panicky.

"I heard a shot…" Her voice trailed off. Her steps slowed. She stared at Julianne, who stared back.

Zach hadn't said he'd brought someone with him. Had he rescued her? Was that where he'd been? He hadn't been home long enough to tell her anything.

Julianne tried to smile, feeling a need to put the stranger at ease. "We don't usually have much excitement around here."

The woman's gaze shifted to Mrs. Moody and back

again. "That's good to know. Um, you don't think someone should see what's happening? Check to see if someone needs medical care?"

"They wouldn't want us to interfere," Mrs. Moody stated, although she moved as if to open the door.

"Can't we look out your bedroom window?" Julianne asked. "We might see something."

The door opened then. A disheveled man, fury in his eyes, stumbled in, apparently shoved from behind. Zach followed, gripping the man's arm. Mr. Moody brought up the rear.

Julianne did a quick visual survey of her husband but couldn't see any injury. The intruder, however, showed signs of the dogs' diligence, as his clothes were ripped. She didn't see any blood.

Zach's gaze went from Julianne to the woman. "Have you—?"

She shook her head.

Julianne went on full alert. What was going on? What secret were they keeping? Did it have anything to do with the man, who looked like he'd swum to the island? Impossible, of course, but he gave the appearance of it.

"I'll be right back. Don't go anywhere," Zach said to no one in particular. He dragged the man off with him, Mr. Moody following.

The women stood awkwardly for a minute, then Mrs. Moody said she would make hot cocoa and busied herself at the stove.

The stranger, her hands clenched in front of her, smiled at Julianne.

"Zach brought you with him tonight to the island?" Julianne asked.

"Yes."

"Did he…rescue you?"

"In a way."

Mrs. Moody clanked a spoon against the pan she was using to heat the cocoa. "Can I fix a plate of cookies for you?" she asked, her voice harsh.

Julianne frowned at her tone. "I'll do it. Looks like we'll be up for a while." She lifted the lid on the Casper the Ghost cookie jar, the only bit of whimsy in the entire castle, and pulled out some chocolate chip cookies Mrs. Moody had made that afternoon. She set the plate on the kitchen table, then got out enough mugs for everyone.

All the while she felt the stranger's eyes on her. It was downright creepy. And a little odd to have three women in a kitchen and no one talking, not even about the weather, although Julianne got the sense that the woman wanted to say something.

The uneasy silence almost sent Julianne in search of Zach, except that she knew he wouldn't be pleased if she went after him. Mrs. Moody filled five mugs. The men returned, without their prisoner.

"Do we have a dungeon?" Julianne asked, trying to lighten the gloom.

"As a matter of fact."

"You're kidding!"

"No." He reached for the mug that Mrs. Moody extended toward him. "He's Jacob's father, John Munson."

"Baby Jacob?" Julianne asked. "How did he get here? How did he even know to come…" Her voice faded as she realized she shouldn't be asking questions in front of the stranger. But who had fired the gun? "Are the dogs okay?"

"They're fine. Heroic. He shot at them and missed. Or

one of them jumped him and deflected his aim. I don't know. It happened before I got there. And I don't know yet how he got here. He's not talking."

Mr. and Mrs. Moody quietly left the room, mugs in hand. Zach put a hand on Julianne's shoulder. "I wanted to wait until morning to give you your gift by the Christmas tree." He glanced at the woman.

Julianne was frightened now. He wasn't acting like himself. And the woman made her nervous. Was he sending her away? Ending the marriage? Had he found someone to take her in, someplace safe? He'd stopped making love to her. He had called her only once, and that conversation was cool and impersonal. She shook her head and took steps back, needing to get away, not wanting to know.

"Where are you going?" he asked.

She didn't even know where. There wasn't anyplace to go. To hide. They had a dungeon!

"You don't have any idea who I am?" the woman asked.

Julianne shifted her gaze to the woman. Fear like none other she'd known dove feet first into her, landing hard, knocking the wind out of her. The intensity in the woman's eyes scared her speechless.

"I'm your mother."

Shock zapped Julianne in the midsection. She shook her head.

"Yes. Your husband tracked me down."

"Take her back," Julianne ordered Zach, looking straight at him, not wanting to see the woman who'd abandoned her. "I don't want to know her."

"Listen to what she has to say."

"Why should I? She left me. Left me—" she pounded a fist on her chest "—with *him*. My father."

"I didn't leave you," her mother said, moving closer.

"Liar." It was hard to breathe. Hard to focus.

"Julianne." Zach's voice soothed. "She's telling the truth. She didn't leave you." He set his hands on her shoulders. "Your father kidnapped you and your brother. There are police reports."

Julianne's world tilted, tipped...tumbled. She was aware of Zach putting his arms around her, supporting her as her legs gave way. Nausea threatened. Kidnapped? No. *Yes*. It made sense. It made too much sense.

"Sit down," Zach said, as her mother dragged a chair behind her, then kneeled in front of Julianne. The woman started to reach out, but instead curled her hands into fists.

"I'm sorry you're going through this," she said. "And so sorry you've lived this lie all your life, Tricia." She put a hand to her mouth. "I mean, Julianne."

"My name is Tricia?"

"Patricia Ann Columbus."

Julianne repeated the name. It rang no bells. "He called me Venus."

"Zach told me."

"My brother's name? Nico?"

"Close. Nicholas. Nicky, though."

"And your name?"

"Monica."

"He said it was Paris." Julianne's throat burned. Her mother hadn't left her. It must be the truth or Zach never would have brought her. "You tried to find me?" she asked, the words scraping along her aching throat.

"Forever. That's why Zach found me so easily. I kept my name out there, in case you looked for me. He found your original birth certificate, the real one."

Julianne started to cry. Monica reached out, tentatively. After a moment Julianne leaned forward, put her head on her mother's shoulder and let the tears come. Arms came around her, strong, comforting, secure. Her mother was crying, too. They talked without making much sense. Fragments of sentences, emotion long denied, hope long buried. She felt her mother's lips against her hair, her temple, her cheek.

When they released their grips and leaned back from each other, Julianne saw that Zach was gone.

They never went to bed. They sat on the sofa in the living room and talked, tripping over each other's sentences, sometimes sad, sometimes angry, but touching. Always touching. For twenty years they'd been denied each other. It would take time to catch up.

Julianne would never be able to thank Zach enough. But she would try.

Sixteen

Zach went downstairs quietly the next morning. Voices drifted up the staircase—Julianne and her mother, still talking after seven hours or so.

He walked into the room. Julianne's face lit up, even as she looked exhausted. She climbed off the sofa and hurried toward him, hugging him.

"Thank you, thank you, thank you. I've never had a better Christmas present." She leaned back, her eyes sparkling, her body pressed against his.

"You're welcome." What more was there to say? He knew it was going to change everything between them now. He'd known it before he tracked down her mother, but he'd done it anyway. Because it was the right thing to do. Regrets were ridiculous. She was happy. That was all that mattered.

Monica stood. "I'm going to take a shower." She gave

Zach a curious look as she passed by, as if sensing his hesitation around Julianne now.

"So," he said, putting his hands on her waist and moving her back. "What are we calling you?"

"What do you want to call me?"

"You don't have a preference?"

"I never liked Venus. Tricia doesn't feel…comfortable. Julianne seems to fit."

"It's not everyone who gets to choose their name." He walked to the tree and admired how she'd decorated it, how homey it looked. Long strings of popcorn wound around all the branches.

"Hannah helped," Julianne said, coming up beside him. "Not with the decorating but stringing the popcorn." She touched his arm. "What's wrong, Zach?"

What he had to say could wait. They could have Christmas Day together.

"Nothing. There's nothing." He brushed her hair from her face, the face he'd come to enjoy looking at, with its ever-changing moods and ever-present beauty. "Maybe you should take a nap."

"I couldn't sleep. But I'll shower and dress. There are presents to open."

He nodded. After a moment she stepped away, hesitance and bewilderment on her face.

He headed toward what he called the dungeon, which was just a basement without windows and set up to be a holding cell, including a toilet and sink, just in case. They'd never needed it until now. John Munson would be transported to another location and turned over to the FBI. He'd been out on bail. He'd skipped. Zach hoped Munson would be locked away for a long time, and baby Jacob would be safe, wouldn't grow up as Julianne had, believing her mother hadn't wanted her.

Munson's punishment would depend on how good his lawyer was. Munson could even be out on bail tomorrow. Kidnapping his own child hadn't been an act of desperation or concern for Jacob's welfare but an attempt to hurt Jacob's mother after she'd asked for a divorce.

As it had been with Monica Columbus and her husband, Julianne's father.

When Zach had tracked down Monica in her kitchenware shop in Newport Beach, not even thirty miles from where Julianne had been living for twenty years, he hadn't asked two questions of her before he knew the truth of what had happened. He'd been party to many reunion scenes, with most recoveries being resolved in days. Only one case had stretched out more than a year, and that had ended in tragedy.

But the scene with Monica would stay in his memory forever. Seeing her absolute joy and relief that her daughter was alive and well, had reinforced the importance of his work, strengthening his resolve to keep going, no matter how many times he failed. Every rescue seemed more personal now. He wouldn't forget Julianne's reaction, either. He'd been privileged to be part of it.

Zach unlocked the basement door. With a roar Munson lunged for Zach, who sidestepped him, grabbed him from behind and shoved him into the wall, locking one arm behind his back.

"Give me a reason," Zach said in his ear, applying enough pressure to the man that he swore. "Give me one reason."

Mr. Moody came in carrying breakfast. He said nothing, but he made his point. *Don't be stupid.*

"How did you find me?" Zach asked Munson.

At first he thought Munson was going to stay silent, but he finally smiled, maliciously. "My *wife* called her mother as soon as she heard Jacob had been stolen from me. Even her mother believes Jacob is better off with me. I'll get him back. I'll prove she's an unfit mother."

Of all the possibilities, Zach hadn't considered that. Maybe he was wrong. Maybe Jacob was better off with his father—

No. Somehow Munson had brainwashed Jacob's grand-mother into thinking he was the good guy, and that it was her daughter who was not a fit mother. It made Zach doubly glad that he'd secured a completely safe hiding place for Jacob and his mother. She'd been told not to contact anyone, but that was after she would've made the call to her mother. He needed to find out if she'd called her mother again. She might have to be moved again, and reminded not to make contact.

He was glad to know there wasn't a flaw in his operations.

But there was another issue, an even bigger one. Munson would talk. The FBI would question, would be *required* to question him instead of ignore him, as they'd done in the past. An official complaint would change everything.

Would Zach need to find a new base of operations? Or worse, would he be charged himself, as he'd always feared, prepared for? He was especially grateful now that he'd forced Julianne to marry him, protecting her from testify-ing. But there was Hannah to consider. And the Moodys. And almost everyone else on the Prom. Survivors, warriors, mourners.

By the time Zach returned to the living room, Monica was there enjoying a mug of coffee. Christmas carols played from overhead speakers. The fire crackled in the enormous hearth. A scene straight out of Norman Rockwell, even if a slightly skewed version of one of his home-and-hearth paintings.

Zach took a seat opposite...his mother-in-law, he realized. "Are you going to get in touch with your son now?"

"Not until after his trial. A reunion with him would be much more complicated than the one last night."

"She's happy."

"Blissful, I think, like me."

"You still plan to leave tonight?"

"I don't have a choice"

"You're *leaving?*" Julianne stood in the wide doorway, anguish in her voice. She'd dressed up for the occasion in a red sweater with white trim at the collar and cuffs, black wool pants, and snowflake earrings.

Monica moved toward her. "I have to open the shop tomorrow morning. There's huge business the day after Christmas. Returns, exchanges and gift cards to be redeemed."

"When can you come back?"

Zach heard a bit of panic in her voice, as if she thought that if her mother left, she wouldn't see her again.

"After the holidays, when things slow down. Honey, I promise we'll talk every day. I'll come back as soon as I can get free."

She hugged Julianne hard. Zach saw her squeeze her eyes shut. A light went out inside him, one she'd brought with her.

A minute later she seemed her old, lively self—or tried to be, anyway. "Don't go anywhere, okay?" she said to Zach. "Not for any reason."

"Barring natural disaster or enemy sieges, I'll be here," he said.

He assumed she had a present for him, something too big to wrap. He wandered to the fireplace, held out his hands to its warmth. He was aware of Monica's quiet presence and wondered what she was thinking. Because he was afraid he knew the answer, he didn't ask. Yes, he'd been too distant from Julianne. There was good reason for it.

"You can turn around."

Hannah stood with Julianne just inside the door. His sister clung to his wife. She seemed to be hyperventilating, but then she smiled.

"I have a present for you," Hannah said to Zach. "I'm not sure I can walk that far to give it to you."

Jarred out of his shock, he rushed to her, grabbed her in a hug and held on. She was laughing and crying. Then he hooked an arm around Julianne, bringing her into the embrace. "Thank you," he murmured. "Thank you."

"I really did bring you something," Hannah said, wiping her cheeks. "Here. Open it."

She shoved a package in his arms. He could tell by the size and shape that it was framed art, but he was unprepared for the subject—Julianne, happy and smiling, the view out the tower window behind her. Although penned in black ink she looked colorful. Full of life.

She looked even happier now, if that was possible. Her eyes sparkled with shimmering tears. Her mouth stretched wide in a grin.

Full of life, he thought again. Life that was being held back and dulled by living on the Prom in such isolation. She'd told him before that she had a plan. He'd never asked what it was.

"It's beautiful," he said to Hannah sincerely, while his thoughts flew in all different directions. "You captured her."

"I did!"

He nodded and smiled.

"Breakfast is ready," Mrs. Moody said from behind them.

"Are you joining us?" Zach asked his sister, who seemed to have matured and yet was more innocent at the same time.

"I'll try."

The Moodys ate with them in the dining room. The discussion turned nostalgic, happy memories of Christmases past, avoidance of anything sad or painful, even though they'd all had their share of that.

Julianne fell asleep at the table, her chin dropping against her chest. Tenderness rose up in him. He moved quickly and quietly to scoop her into his arms.

"What are you doing?" she asked, but put her head on his shoulder.

"It's time for a nap."

She yawned. "Okay."

He didn't look at the other faces as he left, knowing he would see smiles all around. In their room he laid her on top of the comforter, then pulled the other half over her and tucked her in.

"Don't let me sleep too long," she said, her eyes closed.

He kissed her forehead. "A couple hours."

"Okay. Thank you for finding my mother."

"Thank you for giving me my sister back."

She smiled, then she was out cold. He pulled up a chair and watched her, images of the past month running through his head. Her belligerence when she'd first arrived and he'd been slow to introduce himself. Her relentless good cheer. Her independent streak. Her curiosity, even though it had gotten her into trouble now and then. The grateful but embarrassed look on her face when he'd found her and the dogs when she was lost in the rain. Her attempts not to marry him. Her face when she climaxed. Her visible relief last night when he'd come through the door, unharmed. Seeing her break down upon meeting her mother. Her happiness and pride at Hannah leaving her self-imposed prison and joining the family.

Family.

Families loved. Made sacrifices. Held tight. Let go. Endured.

There was no single definition of family. Two could be a family as easily as four or six or eight. The only requirement was an unbreakable bond, whether by blood or choice.

Zach shoved himself up and walked to the window overlooking the land. His land. Not exactly a place to raise a family.

He'd forgotten to use a condom the last time they made love, but what were the chances that one time, one mistake, could result in a pregnancy? Low odds, he thought. He hoped.

He left the room then, knowing what he had to do—Christmas or not.

Seventeen

Julianne awoke slowly, holding onto the remnants of a dream in which she'd just told Zach she was pregnant. He'd whirled her around and around then kissed her and held her and told her she was beautiful. "I love you," she'd said. Then she woke up, the dream unfinished.

She did love him. She had for a while, she just hadn't acknowledged it. But her fear when she thought he'd been shot last night had put her feelings for him in stark relief, like a black silhouette on white paper—visible, tangible and true. Even though it changed every plan she had.

She sat up, hugging her joy to herself, then she saw him sitting on the window seat.

"Hi," she said shyly, savoring her new awareness of him.

"Hi."

She looked at the clock and gasped. "You weren't supposed to let me sleep this long. Four hours! Zach. I want to spend time with my mother before she leaves." She jumped out of bed, grabbed her shoes.

"There's no hurry."

"Of course there's a hurry."

"No."

Alerted by his tone of voice, she stopped in the middle of putting on her second shoe. "Why not?"

He approached her, his expression serious. He didn't touch her. "I think you should go with your mother."

She shivered. The words were ominous, unexpected and cold. "Why?"

"You need time together. Time to catch up and establish your relationship."

She tried to stay calm, while inside her the turbulence whirled at a faster and faster pace. "How can I? I'm here because I need to be in hiding."

"I've already handled that. You'll have a full-time bodyguard for now."

Her throat closed. Why was he being so icy toward her? What had changed? "I'm your wife. My place is with you."

"Alibis and appearances," he said.

"Doesn't it matter that we—" she gestured toward the bed "—you know. We can't get an annulment anymore. And we haven't talked about this, but now with this whole business with Jacob's father, won't you be questioned?"

"You don't need to worry about it."

"Don't treat me like a child, Zach." Her heart, so filled with happiness just moments ago, seemed to shrink into a tight, fiery ball. He'd run hot and cold with her, but she hadn't expected him to be cruel. "If you want me to go, you only have to say so. I wouldn't stay where I'm not wanted. Don't make up excuses."

"I want you to go."

Fury rose inside her, obliterating the pain. "Will you tell Hannah or shall I?" she asked.

"I will." He headed toward the door. "You should pack."

"I don't understand how you can change so fast."

"I haven't changed, Julianne. Circumstances have changed. I gave it a lot of thought while you were asleep. You have your mother now."

"Husbands come before mothers."

"Real husbands, perhaps."

They stared at each other. After a moment she walked up to him. If she could get close enough she could see the truth. She didn't believe he could change that fast. Something had happened while she napped, but what?

She stood in front of him. His gaze never wavered.

"I don't think you want me to go," she said, hoping.

"Don't make me repeat myself."

"You can't treat me as tenderly as you did this morning then dump me like that. What are you afraid of?"

"I have nothing more to say."

She put her hands on his chest. She didn't want to cry in front of him…. Well, why not? Shouldn't he see the truth? She stopped fighting the pain and hurt of his dismissal. If she had to leave, she would leave with honesty.

"I think you're afraid of me," she said. "Of your feelings for me. Of my feelings for you. You've wallowed in your own pain and guilt for so long you don't know how to let yourself be happy."

"Why shouldn't I feel pain and guilt? My brother died. My sister checked out of the world for thirteen years."

"Thirteen years in which you've made amends in ways

beyond what most people could. You've earned some happiness yourself, don't you think?"

"That implies you make me happy."

He might as well have stabbed her in the heart. "I think I did. I think everyone in this castle was happier because of me."

"I'll grant that you brought changes. Please don't drag this out." He moved her back.

"Does my mother know I'm coming with her?"

"Yes. She agrees it's the right decision."

What mother wouldn't? They'd been apart for twenty years. Of course she would want to spend time together. But did she know Zach meant it was permanent, not just a kind gesture from a husband to his wife?

"All right, Zach." She let the tears fall then. No matter how hurt or angry she was, she loved him and wanted to stay with him, to work things out. She didn't want him to forget that, even if she couldn't give him the words.

"It's really for the best," he said.

"For you."

"And you. You'll see." He left.

She refused to give in to the overwhelming anguish. Her movements abrupt and shaky, she got busy packing the most necessary items. Everything else could be boxed and shipped later. She had to find a way to put on a happy face while she said goodbye to everyone, not let them know how devastated she was, let them think she was coming back after she and her mother had time to reconnect.

Julianne heard a helicopter circle overhead, then land. So, they would be given star treatment. No boat ride but a quick escape, probably to a private jet to take them the rest of the way.

She carried her own suitcase downstairs and set it next to her mother's. Mr. Moody picked up both pieces of luggage. He gave her a smile.

"We'll miss you," he said.

It was almost her undoing. What a change from the reticent man she'd met her first day. Yes, she had brought changes to this place. Good ones.

She hugged him. Her eyes filled. Mrs. Moody embraced her, too.

"Now, now," she said, patting Julianne's back. "You'll be home before you know it."

Julianne nodded. Zach rounded the corner and came toward them. A door opened and closed down the hall. Her mother approached.

"I haven't said goodbye to Hannah," Julianne said, wiping her eyes.

"I'm here."

They all looked toward the top of the stairs. Hannah stood with a suitcase in her hand.

"I'm coming with you," she said, starting down the stairs.

Julianne spun toward Zach. He'd gained and lost his sister in the same day. And his wife.

"Are you sure?" he asked.

"I'll come back when Julianne does. I think I need to do this, though." Her voice got a little shaky. "Thank you for taking such good care of me all this time."

He hugged her. Julianne didn't know what she would do if he hugged her. Could she hold herself together?

"The helicopter is waiting," he said.

In the rush of getting to the helipad and stowing the luggage, Julianne lost her ability to think clearly. She followed along, barely hearing their conversations—Hannah's excitement and her mother's pleasure. She had fallen into a pit so deep she didn't know if she could find her way out.

There was no light to guide her.

Her mother boarded first. Hannah followed. Julianne didn't move, couldn't move. If she got on that helicopter she would be resigning herself to her marriage ending. No matter what the circumstances of how it came to be, she'd come to believe it was real. Based on love. Based on commitment.

Mrs. Moody said something about leaving them alone to say goodbye. Julianne saw Zach move close to her. She wanted to fling herself in his arms. She stayed rooted in place.

"Is it okay that Hannah comes along?" he asked.

She nodded.

"I know this is hard—"

"You have no idea," she interrupted, finding her voice at last. "You ruined everything good and wonderful that I found here. I don't even know what was true and what wasn't. What was a game on your part, and what was real. I'm much worse off than when I arrived. I will never forgive you for that." She lifted her face a little higher. "You were supposed to keep me safe. You caused more harm than anything my brother could've done. Goodbye, Zach."

The pilot awaited her, assisting her into the chopper. She never looked back.

"I promise I won't keep you too long," her mother said, making her own assumptions about why Julianne was upset. "It was nice of him to share you."

At some point Julianne would have to tell her what had happened. But she didn't need to put a damper on their reunion—or Hannah's reentry into the world.

She gave in and looked out the window as the helicopter ascended. Zach still stood there, an arm raised to block the turbulence from the blades. Then he waved. To whom, she wasn't sure.

She gripped her hands together and faced forward.

One chapter ends and another begins.

She should've been good at that by now.

Eighteen

"Thank you. And please come again." Julianne smiled at the departing customer in her mother's shop. The smile was automatic, even though she was exhausted. She looked at the clock. Five minutes to closing, and three customers still roamed the store, not looking anywhere near ready to pay for their purchases.

Hannah, on the other hand, looked ready to go another three hours. Julianne had never seen anyone take to a job as Hannah had. In the six weeks they'd been working with Monica in the shop, Hannah had learned more about cooking than Julianne had in her entire life.

Her mother rounded the counter and leaned close. "It's over."

"We're closing early?"

"The trial, honey. The trial's over."

Julianne's heart pounded. "Nico?"

"Guilty on all counts."

"What does it mean?"

"His lawyer said he'll probably get seven to ten years." She lowered her voice. "Nicky's passed the word that you're to be left alone."

"Can I believe that will happen?"

"Apparently so. He's also been ordered to make restitution to some victims, particularly your friend in San Francisco. There are ways around that, of course, but he says going to do it. *And*, honey, he also says there's a trust fund in your name that should've come to you when you turned twenty-one."

Shock took her breath away. "How much?"

"I guess I'm ready," a customer said, dumping her items on the counter.

Julianne would have asked Hannah to ring her up, but she was busy with another customer, talking her into a full set of oven-proof skillets. Monica, meanwhile, grinned, enjoying herself at Julianne's expense.

How much?

Monica kept her waiting until the last customer left and the door was locked. She and Hannah would go to the back room to take care of the day's receipts while Julianne straightened the shelves.

"Two million," Monica said, her excitement barely contained.

"Dollars?"

"Apparently."

Hannah looked from one woman to the other. "What's going on?"

"My father apparently left me a trust fund. Mom, that's dirty money. How can I take it?"

"You want to give it to charity?"

Julianne considered it. Yes. Yes, she wanted to do exactly that, part of it, anyway. "I want you to have half."

"What? No. It's yours."

"Things should've been different. I'm turning half over to you."

"We'll talk about it later." She headed toward the back room.

Hannah grinned. "Zach is going to be so surprised."

After six weeks Julianne still hadn't told Hannah she wasn't going back to the Prom, that the marriage was a fraud. Hannah had made huge progress, but she was still naive. She didn't even think it was ridiculous of Julianne to have stayed away from her husband this long—or that Zach hadn't been to see her either.

Julianne had mastered the art of excuses. And she'd stopped crying herself to sleep.

Why, if Zach Keller walked right through that door right at that second, she'd be able to resist him completely. She would keep her chin up and her pulse under control. Julianne grabbed a dust cloth and walked down the first aisle, her shoulders back.

Hannah wasn't the only one who'd made progress.

Zach stared through the window of the upscale kitchenware store. Closed. He'd arrived ten minutes too late. Then he spotted movement down one of the aisles—Julianne, dusting a shelf.

He felt gut punched. She looked the same but...happier.

She danced as she dusted, and seemed to be singing, too. He'd never seen her that carefree at the castle. He hadn't encouraged her moments of exuberance that seemed to come from out of nowhere then just as quickly disappeared when he squelched them.

He hadn't been good for her. He knew that.

And he was here to set her free. He carried divorce papers in his pocket. He wouldn't keep her from living her life—or from her plan, whatever it was—any longer.

She spotted him and froze, her hand pressed to her belly. Then she dropped the duster, ran to the door, was all thumbs unlocking it. She jerked open the door and threw herself in his arms, landing hard, almost knocking him down.

"You came! You finally came!"

He heard her voice shake, then felt her body follow suit as she cried, sobbed, actually. He hadn't expected that kind of greeting. He'd expected—

He didn't know what the hell he'd expected. But now he was torn between wrapping her up in his arms and never letting go—and giving her the divorce papers and her freedom...

Wait. The minute she'd seen him, she'd touched her abdomen, as if...as if she was pregnant?

And she hadn't told him?

"I've missed you so much," she said, peppering his face with kisses, transferring her salty tears onto his face. Emotional. She was way too emotional. Definitely pregnant. And she'd kept it from him.

"When were you planning on telling me?" he asked, ordered really, as he moved her back.

"If you would've called, I would've told you." She swiped her fingers across her cheeks. Her smile widened.

"Something like that, you should've taken the initiative, don't you think?"

She frowned. "I didn't think you'd want to hear it from me."

"Not want to—? Why wouldn't I?"

"Because you sent me away." Her voice got soft, her frown deepened. "Why would I call and tell you I missed you?"

His mind went blank for a moment. "I meant the baby. Why didn't you tell me about the baby?"

"What baby?"

He dropped his gaze to her belly. She had her hand there again, as if protecting their child. "Our baby."

He saw Monica and Hannah approach. Hannah picked up speed, and threw herself into his arms much as Julianne had done. Julianne stared at him, fury gathering in her stormy hazel eyes.

"What's this about a baby?" Monica asked.

"He thinks I'm pregnant," Julianne said, crossing her arms.

"Are you?"

Julianne's mouth dropped open. "No, Mother, I am not. I have no idea why he thinks so."

Hannah had stepped back and was watching the scene with great interest, Zach realized. And Monica's eyes were sparkling. He needed to get Julianne alone. To finish the conversation. She wasn't pregnant. Wishful thinking...

"That's why you're here," Julianne said, her voice rising as she came to her own conclusions. "You thought I was pregnant. You didn't want me back. You just wanted me because—"

"Of course he wanted you back," Hannah said firmly. "He loves you. Anyone can see that. Why wouldn't he want you back?"

"Did you come because you thought I was pregnant or because you love me and can't live without me?" Julianne challenged.

The divorce papers tucked inside his jacket might as well have caught fire. He started to sweat.

Monica took Hannah by the arm. "We'll leave you to your conversation. Lock up when you're done, honey."

Zach looked everywhere but at Julianne while he waited for his sister and his mother-in-law to go. When the store was quiet, he took a step toward his wife.

His wife.

He didn't have to give her up. Legally she was bound to him. He could make her stay. He wanted her to stay.

"You haven't answered my question," she said. "As usual."

"I love you."

She lifted her chin abruptly, but she also swallowed before she spoke. "That's why you came? To tell me that?"

He pulled the papers from his pocket and passed them to her. "This is why I came."

He expected her to get mad, to toss them back in his face. Instead she read them silently, accusingly.

"Do you have a pen?" she asked.

"I don't want you to sign them. If you do, I understand. I won't fight you. But I don't want you to."

"Why wouldn't you fight for me?"

"Sweetheart, I would fight mad dogs and Englishmen,

and the Cyclops, and runaway trains, and anything else that came along, in order to keep you safe. But I won't make you stay if you don't want to."

"So, you're just giving me options?"

"Yes."

"You won't fight?"

He hesitated. "You want me to fight?"

Her voice became almost a whisper. "I was never wooed, you know. You forced me to the altar. I'd like to be—" She made a gesture of helplessness.

"Wooed."

She nodded, her lips trembling.

"That's fair. Can I take the rest of my life to do that?"

He wouldn't have thought she had any more tears left in her, but they flowed as she nodded again. "I love you, Zach."

He took her in his arms and held her close. He'd missed her. Every day had been hell without her.

"I'm coming with a dowry this time," she said against his chest. "A trust fund from my father. A million dollars. I want to use it to help the victims. A fund separate from yours. One where I would be able to help in a different way." She leaned back. "Are you still in business?"

"My actions are being overlooked. Officially and unofficially. But I'm moving the operation to Seattle." Which was a condensed version of what had happened and all the negotiations he'd endured. He could explain it all later. "Think you can stand living in Seattle?"

"The Prom?"

"Will still be a base of operations, a safe place to come

and go, but I can work anywhere. I've decided it's time to start living."

"I can live with that."

"What about your plan?"

"It keeps evolving. I've decided to keep it fluid, not get locked into any one vision." She leaned back and smiled that brilliant smile of hers. "Right now my plan is to find the nearest hotel and get you naked."

That was a plan he could endorse.

* * * * *

SPECIAL EDITION™

Welcome to Danbury Way— where nothing is as it seems...

Megan Schumacher has managed to maintain a low profile on Danbury Way by keeping the huge success of her graphics business a secret. But when a new client turns out to be a neighbor's sexy ex-husband, rumors of their developing romance quickly start to swirl.

THE RELUCTANT CINDERELLA

by *CHRISTINE RIMMER*

Available July 2006

Don't miss the first book from the Talk of the Neighborhood miniseries.

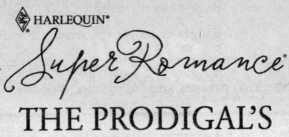

THE PRODIGAL'S RETURN

by *Anna DeStefano*

Prom night for Jenn Gardner and Neal Cain turned into a tragedy that tore them apart. Eight years later, Jenn has made a life for herself and her young daughter. But when Neal comes home, Jenn sees that he is still consumed with the past. Maybe she can convince him that he's paid enough and deserves happiness a second time around.

"Anna DeStefano's remarkable stories of the healing power of love touch the heart with hope. One of the genre's rising stars..."
—Gayle Wilson, two-time
RITA® Award-winning author

On sale July 2006!
Available wherever books are sold, including most bookstores, supermarkets, discount stores and drugstores.

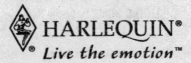

HARLEQUIN®
Live the emotion™

Page-turning drama…

Exotic, glamorous locations…

Intense emotion and passionate seduction…

Sheikhs, princes and billionaire tycoons…

This summer, may we suggest:

THE SHEIKH'S DISOBEDIENT BRIDE
by Jane Porter

On sale June.

AT THE GREEK TYCOON'S BIDDING
by Cathy Williams

On sale July.

THE ITALIAN MILLIONAIRE'S VIRGIN WIFE

On sale August.

With new titles to choose from every month,
discover a world of romance in our books written
by internationally bestselling authors.

HARLEQUIN® *Presents*

It's the ultimate in quality romance!

Available wherever Harlequin books are sold.

www.eHarlequin.com

HPGEN06

COMING NEXT MONTH

#1735 UNDER DEEPEST COVER—Kara Lennox
The Elliotts
He needed her help, she needed his protection, but posing as
lovers could prove to be risky…and every bit the scandal.

#1736 THE TEXAN'S CONVENIENT MARRIAGE—
Peggy Moreland
A Piece of Texas
A Texan's plans to keep his merger of convenience casual are
ruined when passion enters the marriage bed.

#1737 THE ONE-WEEK WIFE—Patricia Kay
Secret Lives of Society Wives
A fake honeymoon turns into an ardent escapade when the
wedding planner plays the millionaire's wife for a week.

#1738 EXPOSING THE EXECUTIVE'S SECRETS—
Emilie Rose
Trust Fund Affairs
Buying her ex at a charity bachelor auction seemed the perfect
way to settle the score, until the sparks start flying again.

#1739 THE MILLIONAIRE'S PREGNANT MISTRESS—
Michelle Celmer
Rich and Reclusive
A stolen night of passion. An unplanned pregnancy. Was a forced
marriage next?

#1740 TO CLAIM HIS OWN—Mary Lynn Baxter
He'd returned to claim his child—but his son's beautiful guardian
was not giving up without a fight.

SDCNM0606